BLIND FLIGHT

Debbie Whitfield loves flying with her Uncle Walt in his aeroplane when he offers her the chance. One day the flight turns into a nightmare when an accident leaves Uncle Walt unconscious and Debbie at the controls, for she is blind!

Her mayday message is picked up by the pilot of a charter flight who gets in touch with the local airfield. Everyone rushes to help – pilots search for the crippled aeroplane, and one of the airfield's finest flying instructors, Mike Griffin, is chosen to try to talk her down to safety before the fuel runs out. But Debbie is slowly being numbed by the freezing air rushing into the cockpit. Debbie has no choice: she must land her plane – or die!

A nail biting hair raiser for readers of 10 and over.

D1382515

Blind Flight

HILARY MILTON

Hippo Books
Scholastic Publications Limited
London

Scholastic Publications Ltd,
141–143 Drury Lane, London, WC2B 5TG,
England

Scholastic Book Services,
50 West 44th Street, New York, NY 10036, USA

Scholastic Tab Publications Ltd,
123 Newkirk Road, Richmond Hill, Ontario
L4C 3G5 Canada

Ashton Scholastic Co Pty Ltd, Box 579,
Gosford, New South Wales, Australia

Ashton Scholastic Co Pty Ltd,
9–11 Fairfax Avenue, Penrose, Auckland,
New Zealand

First published by Franklin Watts,
New York, USA 1980
First published in the UK by Scholastic
Publications Ltd 1982
Copyright © 1980 Hilary Milton
All rights reserved

Made and printed in Great Britain by
Cox & Wyman Ltd, Reading
Set in Linotron Plantin by Input Typesetting Ltd

This book is sold subject to the condition that it
shall not, by way of trade or otherwise, be lent,
re-sold, hired out, or otherwise circulated without
the publisher's prior consent in any form of bind-
ing or cover other than that in which it is published
and without a similar condition including this condition being imposed on the subsequent purchaser.

To Patty, Michelle, and David

1

On this bright Saturday afternoon in mid-October Debbie Whitfield was sitting at the oval table in her Aunt Eva's sunlit breakfast room. In the chair beside her were her warmest gloves, a down jacket, and her new gold and green wool stocking cap. And though she didn't think she would need them, she also had on her lined boots. On the table before her was a steaming mug of hot chocolate.

"Is it too hot?" The question came from Aunt Eva, who was at the counter near the stove, putting the ingredients for two mincemeat pies and two peach turnovers into baking tins.

Debbie put both hands on the table and slid them forward over its polished surface until her fingers touched the mug. She cautiously lifted it to her lips. "It *is* pretty warm."

"You'll need it, though." That was her mother, who was across the room from Aunt Eva putting the lunch dishes in the dishwasher.

"That you will," Aunt Eva agreed. "It may be bright and warm in here, but once you get upstairs it'll be freezing."

Upstairs was Aunt Eva's word for flying, and as soon as Uncle Walt finished making those business calls he'd mentioned at lunch, he was going to take Debbie for a ride in the small plane now parked in its own little hangar on the other side of the barn.

Debbie took another cautious sip of the hot chocolate and eased the mug back onto the table. She felt for the stocking cap and took her time putting it on, carefully tucking her hair in, making certain the long strands were pushed well behind her ears. As she did so, she thought again, as she did almost every time she came to visit her aunt and uncle, how her ash blond hair was more the shade of Aunt Eva's than that of her own mother. Ethelyn—Eth, as everybody called her mother—had hair more like Rick's. Or, more properly, Rick's hair was like his mother's, golden blond.

"By the way," her mother said as she closed the door to the dishwasher, "where's Rick?"

"At the barn, I guess. When Aunt Eva said she'd go riding with him as soon as she had the pies in the oven, he ran out of the back door."

Aunt Eva laughed softly. "I'll bet he took an apple for Ranger."

"And one for himself," Debbie said. Though she was thirteen, two years older than her brother, they played and did things together so often that she could almost guess his thinking. He'd coax Ranger with half the apple now, then keep the other half until they were somewhere on the trail— and feed it to him when he wanted him to run.

Using both hands, she raised the warm mug once more and drained it. When it was empty, she held the side of it to her cheek, momentarily relishing the leftover warmth. "Mum, what time does Dad's plane get in?"

Her mother crossed the room and stared through

the window. "When he phoned last night he said he hoped to make the early flight. Gets in at eight-forty."

"Are we going to meet it?"

"Sure," Aunt Eva said. "And we're all coming back here—"

"We could go on home," Eth said.

"No way. This is *our* weekend, remember?"

Debbie knew what she meant. One weekend each month, her family came to visit Uncle Walt and Aunt Eva, and for one weekend each month they came to her house. Like having two places, without the cost, Uncle Walt said. As far as Debbie and Rick were concerned, it was even better. They really enjoyed being on the farm, feeding the chickens, herding the cows, riding the tractor with Uncle Walt. Almost every time they came visiting, Rick went home saying he meant to be a real farmer when he grew up. Of course, the next time he saw car races on TV, he forgot farming and was absolutely positive he'd one day be a racing driver.

"Debbie!"

She turned quickly. "In the kitchen, Uncle Walt."

"Better slip on your jacket—time to go." He came into the room from the den and helped her into the light garment. "And don't forget these." He handed her the gloves.

"How long will you be gone?" Aunt Eva asked.

"Hour, hour and a half," Uncle Walt said. "Should be back no later than three-thirty."

"What do you want for your supper?"

"We're eating out—remember?" He caught Debbie's shoulder, gently guiding her toward the back door. "I promised Rick we'd have a barbecue at the Rack and Stable."

"You're going to spoil him," Eth said.

"Well, let him," Aunt Eva said. "With Jason and Steve off at the Tech, he needs somebody to spoil. Besides, you haven't eaten there—it's really good."

Uncle Walt held the door for Debbie and took her hand as they crossed the patio to the driveway. He helped her climb into the jeep, then went round to the other side. "What do you want to fly over this time—Paris, Rome, London?"

She laughed, settling into the firm seat and stretching her legs. "How about Moscow?"

"Moscow it is," and with a quick pat on her knee, they started off.

There was one difference, she thought, as they moved down the bumpy dirt road towards the aircraft, about this weekend. This time they'd come two weeks earlier. Because of her. Because of Monday. Monday—when she had to go to the hospital for that operation—

She caught at the thought and shook her head. She'd promised herself she would not think about that—just as she supposed all the others had promised themselves they would not mention it.

Uncle Walt braked, turned the jeep off the road, and stopped. "You wait here while I check with Charlie to make sure he fuelled up the Kadet."

"Tell him hello for me."

"I'll do that."

After he'd left, Debbie eased out and moved to the front of the jeep. With her hand on the warm bonnet, she leant against it, tilted her head until the sunlight fell full on her face, took a deep breath, and sniffed at the fresh aroma she couldn't put a name to. Maybe it came from the hay—she knew they weren't far from the barn. Or maybe it came from the freshly turned earth at the far side of the road. Might even be coming from some late-flowering wild bush that she didn't recognize. But whatever its source, it was sweeter than any perfume she could think of. She brushed back a loose strand of hair and slowly slipped her hands into her gloves.

She was still standing there, face up, when she heard Uncle Walt coming towards her. "All ready," he said. "Let's climb aboard—for that trip to Moscow." He caught her hand and together they crossed the stubble of grass to the little plane. He helped her in, bent over and fastened her safety belt, then went round and climbed into the pilot's seat. He started the engine, revved it up, and made a quick but thorough pre-flight check to be certain that the carburettor heater and magnetos were functioning correctly. "Okay," he said. "Everything's working as it should." He revved the engine once more. And now the aroma Debbie'd sensed moments earlier was gone. In its place was the smell of new seat covers, light oil, and fumes from the engine. She reached forward, letting her hands fall loosely on the dual control wheel. Neither pushing nor pulling it, she held on while she shifted to a more comfortable position. She stretched her legs forward and discovered that it was no longer a strain to put her feet on the pedals.

Uncle Walt eased off the brakes and the little plane shuddered as it began creeping forward. The ride to the end of the runway was bumpier than the short drive from the house, and Debbie was glad when they reached the turning place. Uncle Walt swung the Kadet in an arc, stopped it, and once more revved up the engine. When its sound became steady, he gave the wheel a quick forward motion, then pulled it back. "What time is it?"

"I—I think my watch has stopped."

She didn't know whether it had or not.

"Hope mine hasn't," he said. He made a motion that Debbie couldn't see, then called out, "Two-o-three."

"That's a funny time," she said without thinking.

"When you're logging time in an aircraft, you have to be exact." Again he revved up the engine, except this time he seemed to be pushing the throttle all the way. The small Kadet trembled, the wings seemed to vibrate, and the entire fuselage seemed filled with sound.

Then with a sudden surge, the plane began moving forward. For the first few seconds, it seemed to fishtail, then as it gained speed the motion became straight and smooth. Debbie began counting but she only got to *eight* when the bumpiness ended, the light craft swished from side to side, and they were airborne. They seemed to be hardly off the ground when Uncle Walt nosed the plane upwards. As always, whenever she flew and the plane began climbing, Debbie thought of a roller coaster—the swooping-up motion, the pull of gravity, the kind of sinking feeling in the pit of the stomach. But Uncle Walt did not let the climb remain steep. An experienced pilot—he'd flown spotter aircraft for the army, she remembered—he seemed just as deft with the Kadet as he'd been with the jeep.

He climbed in a circular pattern, and as they got higher, Debbie thought the sun felt even brighter through the wide windscreen. Still letting her hands rest on the wheel, she sensed each turn Uncle Walt made.

"Want to fly it?"

"I wish I could."

"Tell you what, when you're—" he caught himself and in that brief instant Debbie realized what he'd almost said. He started again. "When the weather's right, maybe after Christmas, I'll give you a few lessons. How about it?"

"Do you think I can really learn to fly?"

"No doubt about it. Today, you just keep your hands on the wheel, let your feet rest on the pedals. If you concentrate, I'll bet by the time we land you'll know how to fly."

"Really?"

"Really," he said.

After several minutes, Debbie felt the wheel ease forward and the pedals come steady and even. She supposed they were levelling off. "High enough for a good look at Moscow," Uncle Walt said.

"How high are we?"

"Let's see—we're eleven hundred metres above sea level. That means we're about nine hundred metres above the ground."

"Nearly a kilometre."

"Right—hey, look over there. Geese flying south for the winter."

Debbie turned her head but she could not see. "They're late, aren't they?"

"Maybe not. Maybe they came down from Canada, stayed a while in Kentucky or Tennessee, then decided to go on to Florida." He chuckled. "That's the way your Aunt Eva would like it—go where the sun is."

"I never have understood how they know where to go."

"Instinct. Nothing but pure instinct." Once more he made a slow turn to the right, and this time, judging from the way the sun bore into the cockpit, Debbie guessed they were heading north. "By the way—here, take this headset and put it on."

"I didn't know you had two of them."

7

"Your aunt decided she wanted to listen, too, so I had them installed."

Debbie took the set and put it over her head, adjusting the earpieces to fit over her ears. "Is that right?"

"Yes. Now turn the mike—that's it, the little thing that comes around the face—adjust it so the end is a couple of centimetres or so from your mouth."

Following his instructions, Debbie was reminded of the headgear sports announcers used on television. For a brief moment she wished she could look in a mirror. "What am I supposed to do with it?"

"Nothing right now. But if we need to, we can turn on the radio, listen for other planes."

"Can we talk to them?"

"Yes. But no idle chit-chat." He hesitated for a moment. "Tell you what, though—we can listen," and Debbie heard a light click as he switched it on. "Now, if we make it to Moscow, we'll be able to hear."

"But," and she picked up the game, "we won't be able to understand Russian."

"You're right. You know, maybe I ought to have one of those radio converter things like they have in the United Nations—you know, those things that translate for you."

"Hey, that'd be great."

Except for the sound of the engine and the whispering brush of wind along the sides of the fuselage, Debbie felt as if she were in another world. No sense of being up or down, no sense of motion, no sense of being anything but still and apart from everything else in the world.

She thought about Monday and wished she could stay up here instead. No doctors, no surgeons, no lying on an operating table, no pain, no staying in the hospital—

Almost as if sensing her thoughts, Uncle Walt reached across and patted her thigh. "Nothing to be afraid of."

"What?"

"You were thinking about what's coming up, weren't you?"

"I—I guess so."

"It's going to be all right. Just believe it. There's nobody better anywhere than Craig Smathers. Nobody. Hey, did you know he and I played football in school together?"

You didn't tell me."

"We did. He had a football scholarship—some said he could have gone on to the pros. But he wanted to be a surgeon and was afraid he couldn't make it with a broken finger."

"He was that good?"

"He was. And—uh-oh, I forgot something."

Debbie turned quickly. "Something wrong?"

"No. Just forgot one little thing you're supposed to do—good pilots never forget it."

"What?"

"Trims. Need to trim the Kadet," and without looking in his direction Debbie sensed that he leaned forward. "There's a little wheel—there, now I've got it. When you get to the flying altitude, you set the plane to flying straight and level. Then you feel it to see whether it's going down or climbing. I'll show you—we'll both take our hands off the wheel."

Debbie removed her hands and let them fall in her lap.

"Feel anything?"

"I—I don't think so. Wait—wait, now. Yes—it seems as if we're going down. Now, I'll just turn this a little—a little more—nope, not yet—a little more. Now. How's that?"

"I'm not sure—oh, yes, now I can tell. It's almost like we're climbing just a little."

"Right. You're really getting the hang of it. You can put your hands back on the wheel if you want to."

"Do you mean for it to climb?"

"Not really. But the very little climb rate will be offset when my hands are on the wheel." He made a slow turn, this time to the left. "Some pilots want the tabs set for perfectly level flying, but I like just a little climb." He chuckled. "Safer to creep up than down."

Just then they hit a pocket of turbulence and the light plane seemed to teeter a moment, wobble right and left, then return to a steady course.

"Scare you?"

"No. Felt good." She took a deep breath. "Uncle Walt, do you think Rick will ever want to fly?"

"That's something nobody knows. But I think your mother and dad are doing the right thing, not making him." He hesitated a moment, then added, "You know, fear of flying's a funny thing. I've seen experienced pilots—men who've even flown in combat—suddenly decide enough's enough. I've also seen people like Aunt Eva, stop flying for a few years, then decide they want to try it again. And like it. I have an idea Rick'll overcome his apprehension—if nobody forces him to fly before he's ready on his own."

Just then the radio made a static noise and for a moment Debbie thought someone was about to say something. But the noise disappeared as suddenly as it broke in.

"Something in the atmosphere," Uncle Walt

said. "Tell you what, let's head north, fly up towards Birmingham."

"The airport?"

"Not all the way. Just over Red Mountain."

Debbie felt the plane bank sharply and she found
herself leaning to the right. After what seemed a
few seconds, she felt the left side lower, the right
wing come up, and once more she felt sure she was
sitting level.

"Now, we'll just follow our noses straight ahead
and see if we can—oh, no! No!"

Before she had time to react to his sudden yell,
Debbie heard the splintering crash of something
hard against the windscreen and felt shattered sliv-
ers of plexiglass strike her arms, her shoulders, and
her face. The aircraft wobbled, fell off to its side
sharply, shook all over, nosed down for a fleeting
moment before it vibrated once more, then righted
itself.

And it felt as if all the wind in the world was
blowing into the tiny cockpit.

"Uncle Walt!"

Debbie barely heard his moan above the thun-
dering force of the wind.

"Uncle Walt! Uncle Walt!"

He did not answer.

Frantically Debbie swept her left arm out and
groped about. Her hand found her uncle's
shoulder, followed it down his limp arm, traced
upwards to his face, back down the side of his
neck, felt warm, sticky fluid, paused, fluttered
down once more, landed on something that didn't
belong there—a feather—clutched the feather,
fumbled again and came to rest on the form of
something that definitely did not belong in the
plane.

Suddenly, Debbie knew what had happened.

The wild geese going south . . . one would never make it.

"Uncle Walt!" she screamed.

There was no reply.

"Uncle Walt!" she screamed again. "You know I can't fly!" She brushed her hand across her useless eyes. "I can't even see!"

2

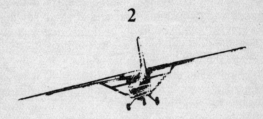

Raw wind roared through the shattered windscreen, scattering maps and loose papers, whistling about the cockpit, filling it with a mixture of sounds that made Debbie think of a barren, snow-capped mountain, away from everybody and everywhere. Biting chill made her cheeks feel suddenly raw. Her jacket swelled. The loose cord to the headset whipped against her arm. Her hands, now clutching the wheel, tightened their grip—

The headset!

She wasn't sure, but those sports announcers didn't seem to turn any buttons, they just talked, that's all they did, just talked. Maybe there wasn't a switch. Maybe when a person talked the microphone worked. She'd heard something about things being voice-activated; maybe that's all it took.

"Help! Somebody—help me!"

The earphones buzzed and cracked. She touched one of them, pressed her left hand hard against the one covering her left ear. But no one spoke a word.

"Uncle Walt, wake up! Uncle Walt, Uncle Walt!"

She heard a low moan, but nothing more.

Birds had no business flying at this time of the year, should have gone south back in September, shouldn't be in this part of the country anyway, nobody cared, just hunters, and if the birds flew this way hunters would shoot them, had no right flying here. And that one had no right to fly through the windscreen.

She felt tears in her eyes, but the wind streaked them back as rapidly as they came, streaked them into her hair and her cap and onto the headset.

"Help, somebody! Please, somebody—help!"

Static cracked once more. But not a voice broke it.

Debbie shuddered. She gasped for breath but felt the force of the wind take it from her. She cupped her right hand over her nose, shielding the wind's harshness, and breathed once more. She fought to keep back the sobs, fought to clear her mind of the grip of panic.

She clenched her teeth and made herself relax her hold on the wheel.

Debbie couldn't see Uncle Walt's face but she knew he was unconscious. Nearly a kilometre above the ground. Nobody knew where they were, nobody could come looking for them, nobody could even hear her.

Once more she took a deep breath, this time forcing out the rush of freezing wind. Holding onto the wheel with her right hand, she caught the headset wire and followed it down to the instrument panel. There her fingers fumbled right and left, searching for the knob. Had to be a knob, had to be some way to turn the radio control, had to be some way to call for help.

Finally, she found a knob and for a moment thought she should take off her glove. But the wind was blowing too hard and she knew that if she took it off and dropped it, she'd never find it again.

Carefully holding the wheel, neither pulling nor pushing, she felt the dial, tested it, and found that it would move. She cautiously turned it clockwise until it could go no further, then she gradually turned it back in the opposite direction. After each move of what she supposed was less than a centimetre, she paused, swallowed, and said aloud, "Help me! Please, somebody, help me!"

But each time she was greeted with nothing except static, static, static.

Once, when she had the knob turned almost as far to the left as it would go, she thought she heard a voice. Jerking her hand away so she wouldn't accidentally lose the spot on the dial, she called once more. This time she repeated a word she'd heard before. "Please, somebody—mayday! *Mayday!*"

But the fuzzy voice she heard did not stop, did not interrupt itself for her cry.

Debbie shuddered all over. Alone. Blind. Flying over somewhere, she didn't know where, not knowing what was wrong with Uncle Walt or who to call or how to fly the plane—

North!

Uncle Walt had said they were heading north towards Red Mountain and Birmingham. But she didn't want to go that way. She wanted to go back to the farm, back to her mother and Aunt Eva and Rick.

She sniffed and tried to remember how Uncle Walt had turned the plane. The wheel, she knew about the wheel, but she'd also felt some kind of pressure on one of the pedals. The left—no, no, the right. That was it. He had pushed down on the right pedal and turned the wheel to the right. And, wait now, something else.

She shook her head, what, what, what?

Her arms—something should happen to her arms. The elbows seemed to have bent when he turned. And the wheel came back a little. Just a little.

She couldn't do it but she had to do it. She had to try.

Holding her breath, putting her right foot firmly on the pedal, she slowly turned the wheel, holding back, but not too much.

Nothing—no, wait—it was turning. The plane was slowly turning to the right.

What had she counted? Eight? Five? Nine? She couldn't remember but she thought it was seven.

One, two—too fast—three, four, five—wait, it was four. That was the count before. Without stopping to think, she eased the wheel back and turned it the other way until it was set with her hands straight across from one another. She let off the right pedal and pressed the left one slightly.

When she sensed that the Kadet was flying straight and level once more, she thought about the way the sun was coming into the cockpit. She couldn't be positive, but it seemed to be coming at a different angle.

She swallowed, counted to ten, and once more made the same kind of turn. This time, when she brought it level again, she tried to tell herself that she was heading back towards home. But she knew that even if she flew right over the farm, even if by some miracle she could get the Kadet right over the runway, she wouldn't know it. And could not land it.

She choked back a sob and once more reached

for the radio. She followed the same procedure she'd used earlier—turn it a four millimetre stop, call for help, listen, turn again and call again and listen again. Once, when the static seemed louder than before, she was certain that she'd located a ground station or even another aircraft. She called for help, she yelled "Mayday!" until her voice was raw, her lungs burning. Nothing.

She had no idea where the dial was set or how many times she had screamed into the microphone when suddenly she found a clear spot on the dial. She listened. There were no voices but something was different, something was special about this one spot. She took a deep breath and held it until she could not hold it any longer. Then, at the top of her voice, she called out, "Help me! Somebody—anybody—please help me. Mayday, mayday, *mayday!*"

Then she waited . . .

Charter Flight 640, bound for Kansas City on its return leg from Orlando, Florida, was cruising easily at ten thousand metres. Jeffrey Billings, the pilot, eased back into his seat, turned his headset mike to the side, and reached for his plastic coffee cup. He took a quick sip, then turned towards Steve Lincoln, his co-pilot. "Going to the game tomorrow?"

"The Chiefs?"

"Sure the Chiefs—who else?"

"I thought they were on the road tomorrow."

"Tomorrow it's the Raiders and Chiefs."

"Hey, that's supposed to be next week—"

"It's tomorrow."

"Are you sure?" Steve pushed aside his own mike. "I've got tickets to that game but I thought it was a week off. And I promised Virginia I'd take her down to the farm." He made a face. "I think she conned me."

"It happens," Jeff said. "Anyway, if you've got tickets and can't make it, I'll take them off your hands. Nan's brother and his fiancée are in town—"

"Help me, please—somebody help me!"

The suddenness of the sound made both men stop talking. Steve's eyebrows went up and he sat forward. Instincitively, Jeff slapped his mike into position.

"Please—if anybody hears me, please help. Mayday, mayday, mayday!"

Jeff touched his headset. "This is Charter Flight 640. I hear you. What's the nature of your emergency?"

For a moment there was silence, then the voice came back. "Huh? I mean—it's me, I mean—are you talking to me?"

Jeff glanced at Steve and frowned. He cupped his hand over the mike. "Did you hear what I heard? Sounds like somebody's not sure what's going on." He moved his hand. "I say again, this is Charter Flight 640. If you're in trouble, perhaps I can help."

They heard a cough, then a quick, choking sob. "Mister, you've got to help me because I'm all by myself—I mean, I'm not by myself, I don't know what's wrong with my uncle—you have to do something. Please—"

The sound broke off once more and again Jeff glanced at Steve. "Whoever it is, she's not making herself clear."

"Sounds scared."

"Sure sounds something." Jeff took a deep breath. "Now—whoever you are, calm down. Try to think clearly. We'll help if we can, but you'll have to tell me what's wrong."

Once more, they heard a soft sob, then a voice said, "I—I'll try, mister, but I need help. Lots of it. I'm in a little plane and the pilot is my uncle and he's unconscious and I can't fly." Another sob. "Help me."

Steve turned quickly about. "It's a kid."

Jeff's experienced eye swept the instrument panel, catching his airspeed, his altitude, and the radio frequency. "Are you losing altitude—are you going down?"

"I—I don't think so. But I can't fly and my uncle won't answer me."

"All right, all right," Jeff said, keeping his voice slow and easy. "Now listen to me. First, what's your name?"

"Debbie—Debbie Whitfield."

"All right, Debbie. My name's Jeff. How old are you?"

"Thirteen."

"Do you know anything at all about flying? *Anything?*"

"I've been up with my uncle before. He lets me hold the wheel, maybe put my feet on the pedals."

"Do you know what those controls do?"

"Not much but some. They make the plane turn and if I pull wheel back, it goes up some."

"Good." Jeff turned to Steve. "Quick—what's the emergency frequency for Birmingham?"

Steve picked up a plastic-coated card and ran his finger down the printed lines. "Looks like it's one-twenty-one-point-five."

Jeff nodded and turned his attention back to his mike. "Debbie, is your plane going up or down?"

"Neither one, I think. But the windscreen is broken and the wind is freezing me."

"Good Lord," Steve said softly. "That child is in trouble."

Jeff nodded but kept his voice low and soft. "Do you know what happened—why your uncle is unconscious?"

"A wild goose or duck crashed through the windscreen—that's all I know. But I'm cold and scared and I needs lots of help. Lots of it."

"We'll help you," Jeff said.

"How?" Steve asked, studying the card once more. "All we can do is hope and pray the thing glides to a clear field before it crashes."

"Debbie, what kind of aircraft is it?"

"I think it's a Kadet."

Steve frowned, seemed to think for a moment, then said, "Hey, ask her what field she took off from."

Jeff relayed the query.

"No field. Not a real airport, I mean. My uncle has his own runway."

Steve's frown disappeared. "I know the craft—they call it a Tahoe Kadet. A lot like a Piper Vagabond except it doesn't require much runway." He tapped the card. "That's a plus—they say those things are pretty good gliders."

"Please—hurry!"

"We're going to help," Jeff said. "Now listen to me carefully, Debbie." He paused. "Are your hands on the wheel?"

"Yes."

"All right. Now hold a little back pressure—do you know what I mean?"

"I—I think so."

"Make sure you don't pull the wheel towards you—but don't let it go forward. And keep even pressure on the pedals."

"All right—but it's cold and my face is freezing—"

"And you're a brave young girl," Jeff said

quickly. "Just hold on. I'm going to switch my radio and call for somebody to help you—"

"Don't leave me! Please!"

"I'm not leaving you. I'm just going to call for more help. But whatever you do, don't touch your radio dial."

"All right. But hurry. Please hurry!"

"I'm hurrying," Jeff said. He reached for the knob but before turning it he read the frequency counter very carefully. "One-one-seven-point-nine," he said aloud.

"Got it," Steve said quickly.

Deftly, then, he turned the knob, stopping precisely on 121.5. "Birmingham Control, Birmingham Control, this is Charter Flight six-four-zero—do you copy?"

Immediately a clear female voice came back to him. "I copy, six-four-zero."

"We just received a mayday call. Repeat—we just received a mayday call."

"I understand, six-four-zero. Do you know the nature of the emergency?"

"Affirmative," and Jeff repeated what Debbie had told him.

"What is the location?"

"I'm not certain, but right now we're ten minutes south-south-east of your city. The young girl's name is Debbie and she's monitoring frequency one-one-seven-point-nine. That's one-one-seven-point-nine."

"I understand, Captain—?"

"The name's Billings, Jeff Billings. And you're—?"

"Mindy—Mindy Jowers." There was a brief pause. "I'm switching to her frequency now."

"I'll tag along," Jeff said. Leaning forward, he carefully tuned the dial to 117.9. "Debbie?"

"I'm here. Did you get anybody?"

"I did." He paused.

"Debbie?"

"Yes—yes, ma'am?"

"This is Birmingham Control—just call me Mindy. Captain Billings told me what you're doing—"

"I'm not doing anything—just freezing and I need somebody to help. Real bad."

"We'll help," Mindy said simply. "You said you took off from your uncle's farm. Where is it?"

"Not far from Redfern—about eight kilometres, I think. But I don't know where it is now—"

"I know," Mindy said calmly. "But think now—when your uncle took off, did he fly east or west?"

"I—I'm not sure. But maybe west."

"Towards the Tri-County Airport?"

"He didn't say."

"If you went west from Redfern, that would be towards Tri-County." Once more she paused. "How long had you been flying when the accident happened?"

"I'm not sure. Maybe fifteen minutes. Maybe twenty."

"But not long?"

"No. But somebody's got to do something because I can't fly and I don't know what to do and we'll crash and I'm—"

"Debbie!"

The sternness of Mindy's voice surprised Jeff and he was about to tell her to take it easy when he realized what she was doing.

"Yes, ma'am." Debbie's voice was still at the edge of panic. "But I've got to tell you—"

"Give me your uncle's name," Mindy interrupted.

"Walter Hodges—"

"All right. Now—Captain Billings?"

"Yes?"

"Can you tell Debbie what to do with her plane for a few minutes while—"

"But I can't do anything!" And now the shrillness in her voice could not be denied. "I can't even see! I'm blind!"

Jeff swallowed hard, turned and stared at Steve. "I don't believe it. Did you hear what she said?"

"I heard," Steve said, shaking his head. "Man, can you imagine what it's like. I've flown blind trainers before. But a kid?—What can we do?"

"Debbie, Debbie," and Mindy's voice came soft and easy—it was as if Debbie had said no more than "I'm cold"—"we'll get you down safely. Believe it."

Steve turned suddenly to Jeff. "Am I hearing what I think I'm hearing? How? How does she think anybody can talk that kid down—"

Jeff put his fingers to his lips. "Shhh. Don't want her to overhear you."

"And I'm scareder than I've ever been."

"I know," Mindy kept her words coming even and reassuring. "Would you believe I am, too?"

"What've you got to be afraid of?" The shrillness had slowly left Debbie's voice, and now her words came clear, though still strained. "You're on the ground and safe."

"I'm afraid you won't like me because I yelled at you just now, and because I can't come up and land the plane for you."

"But you would if you could."

"That I would. Now, believe me—we'll get you down safely."

"But hurry."

"We will," Mindy said. She paused a moment,

then said, "Captain Billings will give you some instruction while I call the Civil Air Patrol and the Tri-County Airport."

Jeff gave Steve a swift glance, then concentrated on the radio microphone. He'd done some instructing shortly before leaving the Air Force. But teaching cadets was one thing. Telling a young blind girl in a disabled aircraft how to stay aloft was something entirely different. He took a deep breath, remembering how little time he had left before flying out of probable range.

"Debbie, listen very carefully. Pretend I'm your uncle, sitting right there beside you. I'm going to tell you how to stay up and fly over the same general area until Miss Jowers gets her people busy. Okay?"

"Okay—but if they don't hurry—it's too cold up here and my hands are getting numb and my face hurts."

"You can do it," Jeff said softly. "I know you can. Listen carefully." He stopped, took a deep breath, and continued. "Keep both hands on the wheel, with just enough back pressure to keep the nose up. Got it?"

"Yes, sir."

"Hey, how about 'Roger'?"

"All right—Roger."

"And keep both feet on the pedals."

"Ro—Roger."

"Now—turn the wheel slightly to the right—a little more back pressure, a little downward push on the right pedal—got that?"

"Roger."

"Now—count to six with me—one—two— three—four—five—six. Now, a little push on the left pedal and a little turn of the wheel to the left.

One—two. Now—tell me how you feel—straight up or leaning?"

"I—I think I'm straight up."

"Good girl. I bet you'd make a real pilot. Sure would like to teach you. Now, count ten—yes, I'll count with you."

When they reached ten, he told her to repeat the steps for the turn they'd just executed. And when she'd levelled off and told him she thought she was sitting even again, he nodded. "Now, Miss Jowers'll be on the radio in a few seconds. What you're doing is flying over the same area—makes it easier for other pilots to find you. And you won't stray too far. Okay?"

"I—Roger."

"You know, if I didn't have all these people with me, I'd stay right up here and help. Even with this jet. But—"

"I'm back, Captain."

"There she is now, Debbie. You're going to be all right—count on it. You call me on the phone tonight and tell me how it came out—will you?"

"I—I guess so."

"Oh, one last thing. I think you said earlier that you were nearly a kilometre up—"

"Uncle Walt said eleven hundred metres above sea level, whatever that means."

"Means if the ocean were right below you, you'd be eleven hundred metres above it. That's a good altitude. You want to keep it—no higher or lower—"

"She can't read the altimetre or the airspeed indicator," Steve whispered urgently.

Jeff nodded. "You'll have to fly by the seat of your pants."

"Huh?"

"That's an old flying expression—something pilots

used to do when their instruments didn't work. You sit perfectly still after each turn, relax as much as you can, and *feel* your position. You know—does it feel like you're leaning forward or backward. If you think you're leaning forward, pull the wheel back just a little. If you think you're leaning back, just push the wheel away from you. But easy."

"I'll try."

"You'll *do* it—okay?"

"I—Roger."

"And don't forget—you're to call me tonight. I'll let somebody know how to get in touch."

"I'll try. And, Captain—Jeff?"

"What is it sweetheart?"

"Thank you."

Jeff rubbed the back of his hand across his face and took a deep breath. "Talk to you later."

3

"One, two, three—"

Debbie counted to ten, made the turn the way Captain Billings told her to, counted to ten once more, and turned once more. Through the earphones, she heard other people talking in the background—near where Mindy was, she guessed. Once she caught the word *Kadet*, and once she thought she heard *crash land*. She shuddered and her fingers squeezed the wheel even tighter.

"Debbie, I need some information—"

"I don't care about information. I just want help—I want to get out of this plane and on the ground."

"I know." The woman's voice was calm and controlled. "And we're going to get you there."

"When, when?"

"As soon as we can."

"I'm freezing—my face hurts and my neck is cold and it's hard to move my fingers."

"Do you have on a jacket?"

"Yes."

"Does it have a hood?"

"No, but I have on a stocking cap."

"Is it rolled down all the way?"

"No—but I can't do that and hold the wheel."

"You have to. Right after your next turn, roll it down. And what about under the jacket?"

"A turtleneck."

"Roll it all the way up—cover as much of your face as you can."

"If I cover my mouth you can't hear me."

"I'll be able to hear you. That mike's very sensitive."

Fumbling with the glove—she dared not remove it—Debbie got the cap pulled down over her face and neck. It was harder, but she also got the sweater rolled up until it covered her chin.

"What's your phone number?"

"Nobody's at my house—my mother's at Aunt Eva's."

"Your Uncle Walt's home?"

"Yes. The number's 764–4133."

"Can you describe your plane?"

"White body, red wings and tail." She made another slow turn and was beginning to turn the wheel to the left once more when a sudden lull in the wind made the plane seem to drop. She screamed and jerked the wheel hard to the left.

"Debbie?"

"It fell! It just fell!"

"Is it—is it straight now?"

"I don't know. I think it is."

"Good. Now listen carefully. We're going to find you—I think we've picked you up on radar but I'm not sure. But we'll locate you, count on it. Then the best instructor we can find will talk you down—"

"You mean *land* the plane?"

"Yes."

"I can't. I don't know how. Don't you understand—I can't see anything—not the instruments, not the ground. Not even the front of the plane." Just then a gust of wind, stronger than she'd expected, slammed into the cockpit, turning the headset mike. She let out a little gasp and grabbed for it. She overcounted the straight times between turns trying to get it back in place. "Why can't I just let it land by itself?"

"You can't. The plane'll come down, but no telling where." Mindy paused a moment. "What class are you in?"

"What's that got to do with anything?"

"You're thirteen—that's third form. Right?"

"Yes."

"Are you studying French? Spanish?"

Debbie tried to swallow, tried to wet her lips with her tongue. She could do neither. What French and Spanish had to do with flying, she couldn't understand. "Spanish," she said.

"Did you know how to speak Spanish before the year started?"

"No." She lost count again, but then thought it was seven. "Eight, nine, ten, eleven—wait," and once again she went through the turning motions.

"But you learned it."

"A little." She finished the turn count, released the right foot pressure, applied pressure to the left pedal, and slowly turned the wheel until her senses told her she was level once more.

"If you can learn Spanish, you can learn to fly."

Debbie couldn't see the connection. Spanish was a language, words—nouns, verbs, pronouns, and sentences. It was remembering, but she could remember things just by hearing them, didn't have to move her hands and feet, just sat there listening, memorizing. "I don't think it's the same."

"It's not the same—not really," Mindy said. "But it's learning."

A tight sob shook Debbie all over, and the chilling winds seemed to make the trembling go on and on. "I don't want to learn it—all I want is to get out of here."

"We'll get you out of there. Safely."

Debbie thought about the words she'd overheard on the radio. Her fingers shook against the wheel. "Am—am I going to crash land?"

"What makes you say that?"

"I heard somebody where you are—you know, behind you I guess."

"Don't pay any attention to what you hear." Mindy's voice remained even and soft.

"But I know it can happen."

"It won't—believe me."

"But when I run out of fuel and it starts to fall—and Uncle Walt's just lying there and he can't do anything about it—" She shuddered. "Mindy, please help me. *Please*. I don't want to die today . . ."

Hans Mitterwahl, flight manager of the small Tri-County Airport fifty kilometres south of Birmingham, sat at his desk in the Operations Alcove, checking entries on a stock sheet. A large, balding man whose eyes seemed to be perpetually twinkling, he had not meant to be here this afternoon. Alabama was playing at Legion Field and he'd fully intended using those tickets his son had sent him. He'd be there right now, and never mind the climb to the upper deck of the stadium, if Wallace Dearman, his assistant, hadn't phoned him saying Mary Lou's time had come and they had to beat the stork to the hospital.

He finished the middle column and leaned back,

forcing the captain's chair onto its rear legs. Without looking at it, he lifted the thick coffee mug and took a slow swallow. "Alice," he said, putting the cup back on the desk, "did Smitherman's ever send that new prop for Mr Cody's Cessna?"

The young woman, still wearing the flight coveralls she'd put on that morning when she'd test-flown a new Cherokee, half turned towards Hans, her hands poised above the typewriter keys. "It came yesterday afternoon—"

The telephone's jangling ring interrupted her. Alice picked up the receiver and answered, and as she listened, the expression on her face suddenly changed. "He's right here, Mr Taylor—just a minute." She cupped her hand over the mouthpiece. "For you—Gordon Taylor from Birmingham Operations."

Hans reached across his desk and caught the phone, sweeping it towards him with a quick motion. "Yeah, Gordie."

"We've got a toughie—a young girl in a Tahoe Kadet, blind," and without hesitating, he gave the full details.

"Good Lord. Where?"

"We think we've got the area identified—somewhere between the Redfern community and Tri-County. We're sending one plane down there now—you know Al Snow, with CAP. Thought maybe you could get another in the air." He paused. "Tried to find Davis Brantley or Marion Tillsdale but guess everybody's at the game."

"Want me to take it?"

"No. Better send somebody else—if you have anybody around."

Hans glanced across at the other desk. "Alice is here—" His eyes asked the question and got a responding nod. "She says yes, she can do it."

"Good, good. Tell her we think the Kadet's at about nine hundred, maybe eleven hundred metres. It's white with red wings and tail."

"Hey, that sounds like Walter Hodges' plane."

"It is—do you know him?"

"Not well, but we serviced the Kadet a couple of months back."

"He's the pilot—"

"The one who's unconscious?"

"Right. Tell Alice to get cracking. It's two-forty now and we think they took off about two."

Hans paused long enough to tell the young woman what to look for, then watched as she left her desk and hurried towards the door, slipping her arms into a green flight jacket as she went. "What are you planning?" he asked Gordie.

"First, we have to locate the aircraft. Then we're going to try guiding her to Tri-County—"

"How?"

"However we can. The kid's scared but she obviously has a lot of spunk. She's been turning in a rectangular pattern for the past five minutes— that's how we spotted her on radar."

"And what do you want me to do?"

"Do you know anybody nearby who has a similar plane?"

"Luck's with us there," Hans said quickly. "It so happens we have one in the hangar—did an engine overhaul last week. It belongs to a rancher down near Parker Springs. He was to pick it up this morning but so far he hasn't showed up."

"Whatever you do, don't let it get away until this thing is over. Anybody trying to help the kid'll want that plane handy. By the way, do you know where Mike Griffin is?"

"Probably at his office this time of day. Why?"

"If I remember, he talked a Bonanza down a few months ago."

"That he did—he's the best instructor flying out of this field."

"Get him out there. We'll need him at the field."

"Anything else?" Hans asked.

"Yeah, two things. Get on the radio with us. And pray . . ."

Deputy Sheriff Jim Lacy answered the phone in his usual monotone, "Steele County Sheriff's Office, Deputy Lacy."

"Deputy Lacy, Birmingham Airport Tower, Gordon Taylor here."

"Yes sir, Mr Taylor."

"We've an emergency in your county—at least we think it's in your area," and as he'd just done with Hans, he spelled out the situation.

"Yes, sir." The deputy's voice still showed no trace of emotion. "What can we do to help?"

"Only one thing for now. Ask your patrol officers to be on the lookout for a small plane—white with red wings and tail. We think we've located it but we can't be positive," and he gave the general location. "If any citizen calls in a report about a plane fitting the description and flying strangely, call me right away."

"Will do," Deputy Lacy said.

"Oh, yes, one other thing. Don't you have a citizens' band radio organization down that way?"

"There's a PACER unit here."

"How about getting in touch with some of those people—tell them to put out the word. We need all the help we can get."

"I'll get on to it right away."

"But please—tell them *not* to come to the airport. We don't want any crowds."

"I understand." The officer paused a moment.

"I guess it might also be a good idea to call the hospital, have some doctors ready, just in case."

"Yes, you might do that," Taylor said . . .

Eva started out of the back door, then paused and glanced towards her sister. "We shouldn't be gone more than an hour—much as Rick thinks he wants to ride, he'll be sore if we stay longer."

The pies were on the counter and the oven was off. Eth was at the sink, rinsing the tins before putting them in the dishwasher. "Have a good time—but don't let him try to race." She laughed. "He thinks he knows all there is to know about riding."

"I'll keep him hog-tied. If Walt gets back before we do, remind him to call Reverend Ashworth— They're having some kind of finance meeting Monday night and Walt's committee chairman."

"I'll remind him. Have a good time."

Eth paused and watched her sister disappear through the door and across the flower-bordered patio towards the gravel driveway. Then she turned off the water and was just drying her hands when the telephone rang. Now who, she said to herself as she lifted the receiver from its wall hook. "Yes?"

"Mrs Hodges?"

"She's not in—this is her sister."

"Mrs Whitfield?"

Eth frowned. "That's right. But who're—"

"Mrs Whitfield, you don't know me, but this is Gordon Taylor at the Birmingham Airport—"

"Don't tell me my husband's already there—he wasn't supposed to be coming in until later—"

"No, ma'am, I'm not calling about your husband. But—I don't know how to tell you this—"

Eth leaned against the wall. "Just tell me."

"Mr Hodges and your daughter—are they flying a Tahoe Kadet?"

Her finger clutched at the telephone cord. "No, no—don't tell me they've crashed—"

"No crash," he said quickly. "But there's been some kind of accident."

"Where are they?"

"They're still in the air—"

"Mr Taylor," Eth broke in suddenly, "can you hold the phone a minute—let me yell for my sister," and without waiting for an answer, she hurried to the back door. Opening it, she stepped out onto the small stoop. "Ev! Ev! Come back! Quick! And bring Rick!"

"What's the trouble?"

"Just come back!"

"Coming!"

Eth swallowed hard and returned to the dangling phone. "Mr Taylor, I'm back. You said accident. What kind of accident?"

"One of those freak things that just never happen. But it did," and he told her about the goose, about Walt, and about how Debbie was handling the controls.

"Oh, dear God, dear God—do you realize that child can't see anything?"

"She told us. Mrs Whitfield, that's one plucky girl."

"But what can she do—she can't fly it—"

"We're going to try talking her down."

"How? She can't possibly control a plane. She's flown before and her uncle's let her sit at the controls. But she has no idea what to do. You know," she added without reason, "she's supposed to go to the hospital Monday to have her eyes operated on—some kind of film's formed over her irises and they're going to remove it."

"Then she hasn't always been blind?"

Just then Rick and Ev came in and looked inquiringly at Eth. With a firm wave of her hand, she indicated for Ev to pick up the extension phone in the back bedroom. "No—it happened recently. Came on all of a sudden—last spring just before school finished.

"Then she's flown before—when she could see the instrument panel and controls?"

"Some. But what difference—"

"She has some idea of where the controls are?"

Eth closed her eyes, leaned against the wall, and let her head rest on the side of the china cabinet. "I don't know. I just don't know."

"We'll get them down, Mrs Whitfield. Somehow we'll get them down. But we'd like you and Mrs Hodges to go to the Tri-County Airport—how far are you from it?"

"I don't—"

"I know," Ev broke in. "We're about twenty-five kilometres southeast of it—we can be there in twenty minutes. But what—"

"I'll tell you," Eth said quickly.

"Mrs Whitfield, we'll have a police car meet you if you'll tell us which road—"

Once more Ev broke in. "Tell them we'll be taking State Highway Seventy-nine—we'll go through Joplin's Corner."

"I'll ask them to pick you up there." Once more he hesitated. "And Mrs Whitfield, believe me— we'll have the best people in the area working with us."

"Thank you." But she did not feel reassured as she hung up.

Ev came hurrying down the hall and across the den. When she reached the kitchen door tears were welling up in the corners of her eyes.

Eth turned toward her. "Did you hear?" Her voice was thick and hoarse.

"No—just enough to know there's trouble upstairs."

Eth took a deep breath and looked at Rick. Then with a kind of desperate gesture, she clutched his shoulder and drew him to her. "Trouble—yes," and as quickly as she could, she told them what Gordie Taylor had told her.

"You mean, Debbie's flying the plane?" Rick looked from his aunt to his mother and back. "But she can't—she just can't do that. How can she? She can't even see—" He caught himself and turned his face toward his mother. "What're they going to do—let her crash?"

"Don't—don't *say* that!" And as if the idea itself were the trigger, she turned suddenly toward her sister. "We've got to go. Now!"

Grabbing light jackets and their handbags, both women headed for the door. "Rick," Aunt Eva said, "run down to the barn and tell Charlie what's happened. Tell him to forget everything else and get up here. Just say I want him to stay in the house, to answer the telephone. And never mind anything he thinks he ought to be doing."

"Yes, ma'am." He hurried on ahead, his light blond hair becoming more tousled with every step.

Three minutes later, they were in the Buick, streaking along Route 79, ignoring the potholes, straightening out the curves, and veering close to the road's edge whenever they met another vehicle coming from the opposite direction.

"Boy, Aunt Eva, you sure do know how to drive!"

"You ought to ride with your Uncle Walt when he's in a big hurry—" She caught herself, then took a deep breath. "I don't understand it, I just don't understand. That windscreen shouldn't break that way."

"Geese are big birds," Rick said. "And they fly really fast. I bet it was going south and they were going north. Were they, Mum?"

"He didn't say," Eth said softly.

Sitting in the front seat beside Aunt Eva, Rick had to turn round to look at his mother. Her face was rigid, and when she saw him looking at her, she glanced down. "Mum, it's okay. They'll do something—those CAP pilots really know what to do. And at the airport they'll fix up the runway so that she can land."

"Son, son," his mother said, and now she could not hold back the tightness in her throat, "I know they'll do everything humanly possible. But she's just a child—"

"She's a teenager and that's different. Boy, when I become a teenager, I sure hope nobody calls me a child."

In spite of herself, Eth halfway smiled. "I'm sure they won't. Not more than once, anyway."

"And you know what else they can do? They can put that foam stuff on the runway like they did on one of those television shows last winter—remember? It's like lots and lots of soap suds all over everything. And thick—Bobby Bristoe—you know, his dad's an airline pilot—Bobby told me that stuff's so thick you have to use a shovel to move it after a plane crashes into it."

"All right, all right, Rick," Eth said. She turned her face towards the windows. Two-forty-five—no, two-fifty already. They'd been up about an hour, the man didn't say what time the accident happened but it must have been shortly after take-off. All that splintery glass or whatever they make those windscreens out of, and that terrible wind—

"Did you see what jacket Debbie had on?"

"I think it was the down-filled one," Ev said. "Walt was wearing his, I know."

"Well thanks be for that. But her face, her hands—She did have gloves, though."

"I know she had them," Ev said.

Rick pointed to the citizen's band radio. "Do you think anybody's talking about it?"

"I don't know."

"Maybe they are—maybe they know what's going on. Hey, maybe one of them's seen the plane."

"Turn it on," Ev said.

Rick flipped the switch. "Wonder what channel they use around here."

Ev frowned. "Never turn it on. But I think I heard Walt once say something about seven and seventeen. Make any sense?"

"We'll try Channel 7," Rick said. Deftly he spun the dial, ignoring all the clicks until the green "7" showed.

". . . that's a good ten-four, Bird Watcher . . . the XYL says no more meters, no more antenna wire, no more nothing a-tall till I buy her a new TV. Now ain't that just like a woman."

"Try the other—"

"Break-break, Channel seven, break for a ten-thirty-three."

Rick sat forward. "Hey, I think ten-thirty-three means emergency."

". . . This is Railroad, KHM-8703—I have a 10-33, a real emergency . . ."

A brief pause followed, then a voice said, "You got it, Mr Railroad."

"Ten-four, good buddy . . . somewhere in the county, maybe east or north of Redfern, there's a little plane having trouble—"

"Hey, that's—"

"Shhh," Ev said.

"It's a white 'un with red wings and tail . . . something crashed into it, folks think it was a goose or duck, don't rightly know which, but it knocked out the front glass . . . pilot's unconscious and a blind kid's at the controls . . . it's still up but ain't no telling for how long . . . if you see one that fits that description, call the sheriff's office right away."

"Hey, Railroad . . ."

"You got the Railroad . . ."

"Good buddy . . . Collie Man here . . . where was the plane flying from?"

"Near as I can tell from what folks at the sheriff's office said, the fellow took off from his own place . . ."

"Not a crop duster, is it?"

"All I know's what they told me . . . could be."

"Railroad . . . Broken Arrow here . . . you say the kid's blind?"

"That's what they told me."

"Well, how in cat's hair can a blind kid handle an aircraft?"

"Beats me . . . likely they'll have to call out the rescue folks 'fore it's over—"

"That's enough," Ev said. "Turn it off."

Rick reached forward and clicked the switch. Slowly, he said, "You know what I wish? I wish it was me up there."

"You don't like to fly."

"I know. But Debbie can't see and somebody needs to read all those instruments. And if they try to make her land and she can't see the ground—"

"Let's just wait and see," Aunt Eva said softly.

"Well, I just wish she had my eyes, that's what I really wish."

Eth reached over and patted her son's shoulder. "I do, too—at least, I wish she could see."

They came to an intersection with a blinking caution light. Just beyond, a sheriff's patrol car waited, its roof lights flashing. "Our escort," Ev said. She steered the car to the road's edge, blinked her lights, and touched the horn button.

A deputy leaned out the window. "Mrs Hodges?"

Ev nodded.

He waved for her to follow and pulled out ahead of her. Then he turned on his siren.

"I wonder if that's necessary," Eth said.

"Sure, Mum. Drivers can't see those lights too well in daytime."

Eight minutes later, when they pulled off the highway and onto the road leading to the airport, Eth glanced at her watch. One minute after three. An hour, a whole hour gone by. She didn't know anything about planes, didn't know how long the little Kadet could remain airborne with a full fuel load, didn't know whether—if it ran out of fuel—it would glide or plummet. All she knew was that Debbie was alone at the controls of a little bird-like plane, with Walt beside her and unconscious.

And Debbie not able to see a thing . . .

4

Once Allen Snow cleared the runway at Birmingham Airport, he wasted no time. Making a sharp right banking turn, he climbed as he headed south. Get over the mountains, never mind Tri-County. Anybody taking off from down there would have to fly a different pattern, anyway. He'd head for Redfern in as straight a line as he could, get there, reach an altitude of eleven hundred and fifty metres, then make the big loop.

So much, he thought, for the afternoon's jogging.

Thirty minutes earlier, he had driven out to CAP headquarters, used the locker room to slip into his jogging shoes and warm-ups, and was just leaving by the side door when the Operations Alert buzzer sounded. He stopped, saw that Kelly Jarman was on another line, and grabbed the nearest wall phone. When Gordie'd told him about the girl, he hadn't even taken time to slip into a flight suit— just thrown a jacket on over the warm-ups.

His watch told him it was 2:53 when he departed. At five minutes after the hour, the Cessna was within visual range of Redfern. Allen knew because when he'd made the last two cross-country flights with a couple of his students, he'd used the Redfern Methodist Church and its adjoining cemetery as a prime check-point. Swinging over Redfern now, he set a course south-southwest, then began the wide, sweeping zigzag pattern he liked so much. Reminded him of some of the search missions he'd flown in Vietnam, back in '70 and '71.

Vietnam. 'Nam and jogging. Truth was, 'Nam had interrupted the jogging back in '69—except that then it hadn't been simply jogging. After winning four AAU meets and running enough sub-four-minute miles to qualify, he'd been preparing for the '72 Olympics. He still told himself he'd have made it except that in 1972 he'd been made Operations Officer for the 1456th Fighter Squadron, based outside Saigon.

This was neither the Olympics nor 'Nam.

He reached for the radio dial knob and switched from 121.5 to 117.9, the frequency Gordie'd said Debbie and Mindy Jowers were using. Almost at once, he heard Mindy's voice.

". . . Debbie, at least two planes are already searching the area—and people on the ground are looking for you, too. Right now, you have lots more friends than you ever thought of."

"I'm glad—but I really want to get on the ground."

"Debbie?" Allen said, keeping his voice even.

"Huh—who's that?"

"I'm one of the pilots Mindy just told you about. Name's Allen Snow—friends just call me the Snowman." He paused to do a 160 degree turn to the left. "I just passed over Redfern and it won't before I locate you."

"Can—can you do one of those parachute things like they do on TV—and land in this one?"

"Sure wish I could, honey—make it a lot easier for both of us. But those things don't really work."

"Didn't think they did." She paused. "What are you going to do?"

"First, I'm going to find you—are you still trying to make those turns?"

"Yes, sir."

"Good—good girl. Mindy, what does the radar tell you—am I getting close?"

"Hold it a sec." She was gone from the radio for a moment, then returned. "Are you zigzagging?"

"Roger."

"The controller says you're about thirteen kilometres from her pattern—if we're still reading her flight."

"Which direction?"

"Course two-zero-five—almost due south-southwest."

"Roger. Debbie, I'll straighten out the curves and be with you in five minutes. Maybe less."

"Please hurry. Please, please hurry . . ."

The phone rang and Deputy Lacy reached for it with a sweeping reflex motion. "Sheriff's Office, Deputy Lacy."

"Is this the office askin' folks to be on a lookout for a plane what's doing some doo-dads?"

"We're trying to spot a plane, yes."

"White whatchamacallit with red wings an' tail?"

"That's right."

"Seems like that's what this one is—right above my south pasture—turnin' and goin' straight an' turnin' once again."

"Sounds like it may be the one we're looking for. Where do you live?"

"You know the Cottonwood community?"

"I do."

"My place is about two kilometres due south of the junction of old Highway 60 and the new Interstate highway. Can't miss it, 'specially from the air 'cause right next to it's a burnt off field of pines— some city gus forgot to put out his campfire."

"Thank you for the information—"

"Deputy, 'fore you go, is it true they's a girl on that plane? An' she can't see?"

"That's true, mister—"

"Hankins—Bo Hankins. You tell 'em for me to git that child down outa there, kid that can't see's got no business a-tall tryin' to fly a plane. And, deputy, s'posing she comes crashing down—what do I do?"

"She won't. Thank you, Mr Hankins—"

"Wouldn't be so sure about that, young fella. I seen one three years ago just flyin' along pretty as you please an' first thing you know, whish and bam and there it was, plumb scattered over two good fields of fresh-planted corn."

"I appreciate your concern, Mr Hankins," and before the caller had time to extend the conversation, Deputy Lacy hung up. He waited just long enough for the line to clear, then tried the number Gordie Taylor had given him. The phone on the other end was picked up before the first ring ended.

"Flight Control."

"Mr Taylor?"

"Speaking."

"Deputy Lacy, Sheriff's Office. Got a call from some farmer near Cottonwood—"

"I know where Cottonwood is."

"Said a plane fitting the description of the Kadet is making passes over his pasture."

"Did he give you a fix?"

"Yes, sir," and Lacy repeated the information.

"Good, good—corresponds with what the radar is showing but now we have a specific fix on it."

"Anything else we can do?"

"Right now I can't think of a thing. Wait—if you can have an ambulance on standby—"

"I called for the fire engines right after you notified us about the plane."

"Good, good."

"Do you want them to go to the airport?"

"Might be best—no, wait. Just have them ready to travel wherever we need them. Tell them to wait at the station until we're sure which way the girl goes."

"Right—will do," and without further conversation, Deputy Lacy clicked off, waited a brief moment, then phoned the fire station . . .

Debbie's earlobes hurt, her fingers were numb, her lips were dry, and the tip of her nose burned. Her body ached all over and she no longer tried to control the trembling. She felt as if her hands were frozen to the rim of the wheel; her legs would no longer move freely, and the wind-whipped tears were coating her eyes. "Mr Snow, where are you?"

"Coming closer, honey—coming closer—"

"Al, Alice Palmer here, I'm in the area now.'

"Good—Hans relayed the message that you were joining the search. Anything?"

"Negative."

"Miss—Miss Palmer?"

"Yes, Debbie?"

"You said you were in the area. Are you a pilot?"

"Right now I am. And like Mr Snow, I'm looking for you."

"You can really fly?"

"I can really fly."

"I sure wish I could."

"Honey, you've been flying for half an hour."

"It's not really flying." She took a deep breath and for the first time since Uncle Walt lost consciousness she felt an easing of the tension. "I'm just sitting here with my hands on the wheel."

"You've been making turns."

"That's not flying."

"That's flying," Alice said. "That's just what I'm doing."

"But you know how—and you can read the instruments—"

"Alice," Al broke in, "I think I've got her spotted. Yeah, I'm sure. Debbie, turn the wheel a little to the left, then a little to the right. Good girl—I've got you spotted. Alice, do you see her?"

"Negative—wait. Down there—looks like she's—" she caught herself, then said, "we're too high."

"Right," Al said. "Alice, is Hans on the radio?"

"I am," a deep voice boomed in. "You say you've spotted her?"

"Roger. She's a hundred metres lower than I am. I'm going down now."

"Give me the altitude when you're sure," Hans said.

Something about the way Alice said "we're too high," and that business about her being lower than Al brought the tightness back. They didn't have to tell her—somehow during all those turns she'd dropped down, wasn't as high as they'd been when Uncle Walt was flying. Going down and down, that's what, and in a few minutes she'd be crashing on the ground—

She choked back a sob and shook all over. "Am I going to crash?"

"No way," Al said quickly.

"But you said I was low."

"I said lower than I am. Let's see—you must still be eight hundred metres up."

She'd lost two hundred metres.

The thought made her cry out.

"Debbie!"

"Yes, sir?"

"Something happen?"

"I—I just figured out how far I've fallen—"

"You haven't fallen at all," he said quickly. "It's natural to lose a few metres when you're making lots of turns. Even good pilots do it lots of times." He hesitated. "And it's just as well that you have— we'll have to go even lower when we get close to the airport."

Debbie swallowed. "What's going to happen at the airport?"

"The best instructor in this part of the country is waiting there now. We'll fly in that direction, and as soon as we're close enough, he's going to tell you just what to do to land."

"I can't do that. I just can't," and though she tried as hard as she could not to, she began crying. . .

At the Tri-County Airport, Mike Griffin sat at the controls of the Tahoe Kadet that was parked on the tie-down ramp just outside the maintenance hangar. His experienced gaze busily scanned the instrument panel, his deft hands touched the throttle knob, the flap lever, and the wheel. He moved the controls back and forth, right and left, feeling them respond to each movement. He'd flown a Kadet only once and that was over a year ago, when he'd made a brief trip to Birmingham and back. But his trained eyes and hands missed nothing.

Twenty minutes earlier, he'd been just outside his office and was about to climb in his car when the small pager hooked to his belt buzzed a sharp signal. He had returned to his office at once, where his partner, Clifford Bradley, told him to call Hans Mitterwahl at the airport. Hans had given him the information about Debbie. "Be right there," he'd said. He'd hung up the phone, dropped his briefcase on his desk, slipped out of his blazer and into a jacket that hung against the wall behind the filing cabinet, and trotted to his car. He'd meant to spend as much time with Jason Millican as he could. For two months he'd been trying to get an appointment with him.

But a blind girl in an aircraft, trying to control it—well, there wasn't even a choice.

Mike shifted his long frame in the pilot's seat, stretched his legs, and settled into the semi-slouched position he'd grown accustomed to when he'd flown in combat. He ran his hand through his thick hair, then deftly adjusted one of the radio's headpieces and put it on. He flicked the On switch and spun the dial to the frequency Hans had told him to use—117.9. Immediately, he picked up the conversation between Al and Debbie. When she started crying he cleared his throat and took a deep breath. "Hey, Debbie, you're really not going to fly it—I am."

The crying suddenly choked off. "You? Who're you?"

He told her, keeping his voice soft and low. "All

49

you have to do is move your hands a little. I'll do all the rest."

"But you're not—I mean, where are you?"

"I'm on the ground at Tri-County Airport."

"But you can't—I mean, I'm way up here and you're too far off."

"I'm sitting in a Tahoe Kadet just like the one you're flying. I have my hands on the wheel just like you do—except it's not really a complete wheel—just a piece on the right hand side and a piece on the left. Right?"

"I guess—yes."

"And when you close your hand over the rims, your thumbs are resting on the cross bar, right?"

"That's right."

"Now, take your left hand off and put it on your thigh, with your elbow touching your side."

There was a moment's pause. "It's there."

"Now, let it slip off and fall limply. It should come to rest on a round knob."

"The throttle?"

"Right—you've been watching your uncle, haven't you?"

"He showed it to me once last spring." She hesitated. "I wasn't blind then." Her voice came as a hoarse whisper.

"Wonderful. Then you have an idea which way to move it."

"I think forward to go faster and back to go slower."

"Good. Now, is your hand on the knob?"

"Yes."

"All right—wrap your fingers firmly round it. Never move it until you have a firm grasp—remember that."

"I have it now. Now what?"

"Real easy now—hold the right wheel rim very

firmly and move it up about a centimetre, back, down about a centimetre, then back once more."

"That'll make it turn, won't it?"

"Just a little but it won't change enough to matter. Okay?"

"Okay."

Mike turned towards the small plane's door, now half open, with Hans standing near the fuselage holding a portable radio in his hand. Mike cupped his hand over the small microphone. "If I can give her a little confidence now, maybe we can bring her in. But what happens once we get her to the airport?"

"You bring her down."

Mike frowned and stared at Hans. "Do you realize what you're asking me to do?"

Hans nodded slowly. "There's nobody better and we both know it."

"But suppose—"

"We do what we can."

"Mr Griffin—Mike?"

"What is it, sweetheart?"

"I did it."

"Keep a firm grip on it."

"I have to do that—I think my fingers are frozen to it."

Mike couldn't be sure, but he thought he detected a change in her tone, as if the tension was gradually easing. Perhaps it was because she was doing something, or perhaps it was because she knew Al and Alice were in the area and could see her. But whatever the reason, the more he could get her to relax, the more he could get her to believe in herself, the better were the chances of bringing her down. Safely.

Safely. That was the key word. The miracle they needed.

"Now, keep one hand on the wheel, the other on the throttle. Al and Alice will fly in formation—do you know what that means?"

"I—I think so. That's when three or four planes fly together, like they did in the war."

"Right on, right on. Now—Al, are you listening?"

"Roger."

"How far are you from Tri-County Airport?"

"Ten minutes—right Alice?"

"Ten, maybe twelve. I think there's a crosswind."

"Radar tells us from Birmingham," Mike said, "that you're almost due southeast. And right now we have a fifteen-kilometre-an-hour wind coming right out of the north, no gusting. Now, Debbie, since Al and Alice are right there with you, one of them will put you on course—"

"What does that mean?" Her toned showed her sudden concern.

"It's real easy," Al broke in. "A piece of cake—you know what that is, don't you?"

"I've heard it before."

"Okay. Now—we're heading west so you want to turn the wheel a little to the right, push down on the right pedal—then hold it until I tell you to let up. Got it?"

"I—I guess so."

"You *know* so, Mike said easily.

"I'll try."

"Good girl. Al—go ahead."

"Okay," Al said. "Alice, you're south of her, right?"

"Right."

"Then we'll turn together. Debbie, when I count to three, we'll all turn together. Ready?"

An audible choking sound passed through the microphone, then, "I'm ready."

"To the right, now—one, two, three."

Mike cupped his hand over his own microphone and turned to Hans. "Maybe, maybe."

"And when they get here—if they do—"

"When they get within range—wait, what's their altitude?"

"Didn't Al say something about her being at about eight hundred metres?"

"Right." Mike removed his cupped hand. "Al, might start your descent as soon as you're on the right course. Debbie, when Al tells you, pull back on the throttle—can you guess at a centimetre?"

"I don't know."

"But you'll try, won't you?"

"I'll try," she said hesitantly.

"Okay, Al—all yours. When you're at a hundred and fifty metres let me know."

"Roger. Debbie, ease the throttle back—that's a girl—easy, easy—now, very gently move the wheel forward—not too much—back a little—hey, you're right on it."

"Debbie," Alice said, "Mike won't tell you, but he's helped more than one pilot land when there's been trouble on board. One night not too many months ago he talked down a woman whose husband was sick." She paused. "You can trust him."

"I'll—I'll try."

"Debbie, turn the wheel a little more to the right," Al said. "Now—you're doing fine. Just fine . . ."

Although she could not see the other two planes, the mere knowledge that they were with her, flying in formation as Mike called it, able to see what she was doing and help her fly, made the tightness inside partly go away. But she was colder than she'd ever been in her life. Her hands were numb and tingling, her cheeks hurt, her lips felt raw and chapped, and her body was stiff from sitting so still. Holding the wheel and throttle the way Mike instructed her to do wasn't easy.

But she knew that this was the easiest of all the things she'd have to do. In another ten minutes—maybe twelve, the way Alice said—she'd be flying with them over the airport. And then she'd have to do what she'd never done in her life, what she couldn't do—she'd have to try to land. She didn't like it. She didn't think she could do it.

She had those ten minutes, though, when she didn't have to think about it . . .

5

Hans stepped away from the small Kadet, glanced once more at Mike, nodded, and turned his attention to the sky, staring in a southeasterly direction. The few puffs of white clouds would not keep him from seeing the plane, and he realized that within minutes it would come into view. He also realized that this small airport was not equipped for the kind of landing the girl was likely to make. If she made any kind of landing at all.

He took a deep breath and wished she were going to Birmingham, to Montgomery—anywhere else. Twice before he had watched as Mike talked down planes whose pilots had been disabled, whose controls had been in the hands of inexperienced people. In both instances, however, the individuals were adults. And they had been able to see.

He shook his head and was in the act of lighting a cigarette when the small pager hooked to his belt beeped once, then twice more. Hastily putting the cigarette back in the pack, he switched a knob on his walkie-talkie and brought the instrument close to his mouth. "Hans here."

"Can you come to the office? The girl's folks are here." The voice was that of Lonnie, a young high school student who spent his Saturdays at the airport.

"Coming," Hans said. He flicked the switch back to the frequency Mike, Al, and Debbie were using and turned to the Kadet. "Be back in a few."

Mike nodded, cupping his hand over his microphone. "Want me to tell the girl her mother's—"

"No," Hans said quickly. Then, remembering that his own hand-held radio was now picking up anything Debbie might say, he turned it off and hurried towards the Operations Alcove, wishing that Gordie or Mindy or anybody else were here in his place. At the door he paused, glanced back, then turned the knob and stepped inside.

Before he could do more than introduce himself, one of the women caught at his arm. "My daughter—what is going to happen?"

"Mrs Whitfield—is that correct?"

"I am," she said, then nodded toward Rick and Ev. "My son Rick and my sister Mrs Hodges." She put her hand on Ev's elbow. "What's being done?"

Hans took a deep breath. "Two able pilots are flying with her now—guiding her towards the airport."

"Guiding her? Guiding her—"

"Mister," Rick broke in, "Debbie's blind."

"She told us." He glanced toward the wall map. "Let me show you what we're doing," and without waiting for another question, he led them across the floor. "Right about here," and he put his finger on a small black circle on the map, "that's where we located Debbie. Now, two pilots, like I say, are flying alongside—and one of them is an experienced combat veteran. Mr Al Snow. He's telling her what to do, instructing her in the use of the controls—"

"Use of controls?" Eth turned suddenly. "She can't even *see* the controls."

Ev caught her sister's shoulder. "What he means is, they're coaching her. I know she's aware of what they are—Walt's had her handle them." Now she turned and faced Hans. "Has she said anything about my husband?"

"Only that he's unconscious."

"Mister," Rick stepped closer to the map and pointed to a black "X" mark on it. "Is that the airport?"

Hans nodded, glad for the interruption. "Al and Alice found her near the Cottonwood community. She'd lost some altitude, but otherwise she was doing fine. Considering."

"I know she's on the radio," Eth said, "but how'd she do it? How did she contact you or that Mr Taylor?"

As quickly as he could, Hans gave them all the details he had—the pilot of the charter plane, the radio call to Birmingham Control, the alert request from Gordie. "We don't really know anything more than she's been able to tell us."

"But what can you do—what can anybody do?"

"I bet somebody's going to talk her down," Rick said. "Like they did on a TV programme I saw, when somebody drugged the pilot and co-pilot and one of the passengers had to take over."

"Rick—"

"He's right, ma'am," Hans said. "Within the next few minutes, Mr Mike Griffin will begin telling her just what to do—which way to turn the plane, how to slow it down, how to begin the descent and line up with the runway—"

A sob broke from Eth's lips. "She can't do it, she can't, she just can't."

Rick caught his mother's hand. "She can do lots more than you think. I've seen her—I've helped her. She can use the typewriter, she can play the piano a little."

"But that's different."

"It's much the same," Hans said.

"I wish, I wish, I wish," Rick said suddenly, turning away from them and walking across the room towards one of the huge windows. "If I'd gone with them, if I was up there, I could see—if I just liked to fly."

Hans watched him thoughtfully for a moment, but a quick glance towards the wall clock brought him back to reality. "In minutes she'll be approaching the field. Mr Griffin's in a small plane out by the hangar—a Tahoe Kadet—"

"That's what they're flying," Ev interrupted.

Hans nodded. "He's in the cockpit, and he'll tell her just what to do." He glanced towards Rick once more. "I'd better go back to the flight line with Mike—"

Eth suddenly reached for his walkie-talkie. "Is she on this one now? Let me talk to her!"

"Mrs Whitfield," Hans tried to keep his voice low and controlled, "Al and Mike have got her calmed down. She's paying attention to them, doing what they tell her to. I know she's very cold and very afraid—but if she heard your voice, she might get upset again."

"And it might scare her," Rick said suddenly.

"But I want to hear her voice."

"Better not to," Ev said.

Hans glanced at her and realized for the first time that the women were twins. "I'd better get back to Mike—they'll be coming into sight within minutes now. There's coffee," and he nodded towards the small table behind Alice's desk. "You can watch from the window. But please—don't come out."

"Mister," Rick looked up at him, "can I go with you? I mean, I've helped Debbie do lots of things since she went—since her eyes started giving her trouble. Maybe I can say something to her if that pilot wants me to."

"Rick, I think you'd better stay with me and Aunt Eva—"

Hans studied the boy's face. "I don't know. But if we need to know something about her, you could tell us." He turned to Eth. "He may be able to help."

Eth looked at Rick for a moment, then impulsively caught his hand and squeezed it. "Help her—help your sister."

"If I can."

"Come on, Rick—they should be within sight any time now." Hans nodded briefly to the two women, then started towards the door. "We'll do all that's possible," he said.

"I pray God it's enough," and Eth covered her face with her hands . . .

"Debbie, we're going down now."

"Getting ready to land?"

"No, no—not yet. We're losing altitude so when we get close to the field Mike can see you."

Debbie couldn't stop the trembling in her body and dared not move her right hand from the rim of the wheel or her left one from the throttle knob. Her face was past being numb and she thought the tears had frozen over her eyes. A painful cramp had settled in her left knee, now and again making her foot jerk nervously. The knot at the pit of her stomach was like a fist, growing all the time, and her earlobes seemed to be on fire, they were so cold. When she talked, her tongue seemed to clack against her teeth. "I don't think I can do it."

"Do what?"

"You know—land it."

Al gave a soft laugh. "Anybody who's been flying all over the sky the way you have shouldn't have any trouble at all just putting a plane on the ground. Do you know how many kilometres you've already flown?"

"Too many," she said.

"About eighty."

"I don't believe that."

"It's true. And you only have about fifteen more to go. How about that?"

"I—I guess it's okay."

It was not at all okay. She knew from flying before with Uncle Walt that it was one thing to fly straight and level and make turns to the right and left, but it was not at all the same when time came to land. Uncle Walt always flew in a definite pattern, looking down at the ground to determine which way the wind was blowing—then gradually lowering the aircraft and heading into the wind.

"Debbie?"

"Yes, sir?"

"Mike here—do you have your hands where I told you to put them?"

"They're frozen there, I think."

"Well, don't let them slip off. Now—Al, give me a fix on your location."

"We're approximately three minutes away, altitude about two twenty five."

"Heading?"

"Heading three-twenty."

"Good, good. Now, Debbie, listen carefully. In

about two minutes I'll want you to ease the throttle back, turn the aircraft, and make an approach. Do you know what that means?"

"I think so. It means you're going to tell me how to line up the plane to come down."

"That's exactly what I mean."

"I won't have to go round the field?" She remembered that often Uncle Walt made something he called a down-wind leg—and she supposed that meant flying in the same direction the wind was blowing.

"No," Mike said. "I'll bring you straight in. Al?"

"Here."

"What's the altitude now?"

"Two twenty five, two twenty, two fifteen."

"Good, good. Now, Debbie, when you hear Al say one hundred, don't wait for me—just ease the throttle back one centimetre, then another, keep the wheel steady and keep even pressure on both pedals. Got it?"

"I—I think so. But I'm getting scared."

"You're doing fine, fine," Al said.

Debbie swallowed but all she got for the effort was a quick tightening in her throat. Her tongue seemed fixed to the roof of her mouth, her teeth chattered, and her lips seemed to be stuck at the corners. "I—I don't feel fine."

"Well, just hang on—hang in there—is that what they say nowadays?"

"I think so."

"Okay—Al, how about it?"

"Smooth all the way. We're at one thirty-five . . . one thirty . . . one twenty-five." There was a longer pause, then, we're at one twenty."

"What's your heading?"

"Still three-twenty."

"All right—hey, I think I see you. Yeah, I see you." Mike paused. "Al, come around to two-seventy."

"Roger. Debbie, turn the wheel to the left—not too much, now, and push the left pedal. Easy, easy—hey, hey, you're doing fine, just fine. Now, ease the wheel back till it's even again, a little right pedal—girl, you sure you never flew?"

"I'm—I'm sure."

"Well, you're doing beautifully now. How about it, Mike?"

"I've got her well in sight," Mike said. "Debbie, we're coming in . . ."

Walking along beside Hans Mitterwahl, Rick couldn't help noticing the growing crowd of on-lookers just beyond the airport fence. He knew the man on the radio had said not to come here and guessed the sheriff's office had passed along the same word. But people couldn't help being curious. They just had to see, had to crowd around anything that seemed like excitement, especially an accident. Like people on the highway—no matter how fast traffic ought to be going, just let two cars bang into one another and everybody wanted to slow down and look.

He suddenly realized that most of the people were looking at him and Hans, and he felt his face get warm. Should have stayed with his mother and Aunt Eva. There wasn't anything he could say to Debbie anyway. That man who was going to tell her what to do, he was the only one who had any business talking to her.

He thought he heard the distant hum of an engine and turned to stare up at the sky. "Mr Mitterwahl, is that Debbie and those others?"

Hans stopped and glanced in the direction Rick

was pointing. "Good Lord!" With a sweeping motion, he flicked on the walkie-talkie and turned a small knob. "Tri-County Airport—will the pilot flying south identify himself!"

"Roger, Hans," a cheery voice said. "This is N-3610-Zebra coming at you—"

"Bart—Bart Waverly?"

"Right on—"

"Get out of this area! Now! Go west—we have an emergency. Repeat, *we have an emergency!*"

Rick swallowed and squinted hard. No other planes were flying except that one and those with Debbie.

"Can't, Hans—I'm low on fuel."

"You can't come in here!"

"I don't have any choice," and now the voice was tight and edgy. "Five minutes is all I have."

Rick didn't know anything about flying, never had wanted to go up in one of those things, couldn't help it, just didn't want to. But he understood enough to realize that whoever that man was, he couldn't stay in the air much longer. He turned toward Hans. "What about Debbie?"

Without answering, Hans switched the dial of his walkie-talkie.

". . . We're now at one ten—"

Hans keyed the instrument. "Mike!"

"Yeah, Hans?"

"Don't bring her in yet!"

"What—"

"You'll have to make her circle. No time to explain."

"What's wrong?"

Rick spun about when he heard Debbie's voice coming from the walkie-talkie. "That's my sister—"

"Nothing, honey," Mike said. "We need to

check the cross-winds to make sure you don't get blown off course. Al?"

"Yeah?"

Rick wanted to hear but Hans once more turned the dial. "Bart, bring it in now."

"Dropping in for the approach."

"And Bart, when you hit the end of the runway, taxi to the farthest ramp you can reach. South!"

"Roger—and thanks."

Once more Hans turned the small dial and pressed the transmitter key. "Lonnie!"

For a moment there was silence, then, "Yes, sir?"

"Call J.R. at the hangar and tell him to get a truck to the west end of the main runway. A blue Cessna's coming in low on fuel."

"You want him to fuel it on the runway—"

"No," Hans broke in. "Tell him if the pilot can't taxi, to hook a pull-rope and tow the plane as far south as he can. Just get it off the runway. Fast!"

"Yes, sir."

Rick did not fully understand what all this meant, but he grasped enough of it to realize that the blue plane had to land immediately or perhaps crash on the airfield. He also realized that Debbie would have to turn the Kadet and get out of the way.

Hans again twisted the walkie-talkie dial.

". . . All right, Debbie, you're doing fine, just fine. Keep the left pedal down, keep the wheel to the left like you've got it—that's right, hold it towards you a little and ease the throttle forward."

Turn the wheel, press the pedal, ease the throttle forward—Rick didn't understand what all that meant but he hoped Debbie did.

"How long?"

That was her voice and once more Rick stopped abruptly. "Is she all right—"

"Shhh," Hans said.

". . . Till I tell you to change." Al's voice was so soft and low Rick thought he could have been talking about cutting grass or feeding the dog.

The sputtering of an engine broke through the sounds coming from the walkie-talkie. Rick turned in time to see the blue Cessna drifting down towards the eastern end of the runway, its wings dipping and rising as the fuselage rocked slightly from side to side. "What's wrong with it?"

"Nothing," Hans said quickly. "A little crosswind, that's all." He glanced towards the runway and watched until the Cessna's wheels touched down, then proceeded at a rapid pace towards a small parked plane that, Rick noticed, was just like the one Debbie was in, except it was grey and orange.

"Is that where the man is, the one who's helping Debbie?"

Hans nodded. "Mike Griffin. Probably the best instructor in this part of the country."

"Is he a commerical pilot?"

"Nope. Sells insurance."

"Sells insurance?" The idea didn't make any sense at all.

"That's right. But before that, he was an Air Force pilot. Flew in Korea, Vietnam." He looked toward Rick. "Teaches flying at weekends."

As they drew near the Kadet, Rick paused and stared in the direction of the Cessna, now rolling to a halt at the far end of the runway. A red and blue pick-up was driving towards it, spewing a cloud of dust. That, he supposed, was the man who'd see to it that the blue plane was pulled out of the way.

Hans paused near the Kadet's wing, glanced once at the pick-up, then ducked low and crossed to the still open door.

". . . Mr—Mike?"

That, Rick realized once more, was Debbie, and he very much wanted to take the mike and say something to her.

"Right here, sweetheart."

"I'm scared."

"I'd be worried if you weren't," Mike said gently. "But you're almost round, almost ready to head towards the runway. Right, Al?"

"Right. Tell you one thing, Mike, this little lady's a natural. Debbie, if Mike could have you for four Saturdays straight, you'd be flying without anybody's help."

"That's right, Debbie," Mike said. "Now, ease the wheel to the left till it seems straight across. And a little pressure on the left pedal—how's it look, Al?"

"Right on it—now."

"Elevation?"

"One hundred."

Rick frowned. One ten, one ten—oh, now he knew, one hundred and ten metres. He didn't know much about planes, but he knew they didn't always use the hundreds or thousands.

Hans pointed to Rick. "Her brother," he whispered to Mike. Mike nodded and smiled. "All right, Debbie. Now, here's what we do. Ease the wheel forward, not much, just a little—that's right. And bring the throttle back a centimetre—make it a little more than a centimetre. Got it?"

"Ye—no. No!"

"What do you mean, *No?*"

"I'm scared. I can't do it. I can't see!!!"

6

Mike glanced quickly at Rick and wished the boy weren't there. But he gave no sign. "Debbie, I've landed at night when I couldn't see a thing."

"But you know how to fly!" He knew by the tightness in her voice that she was tensing up again. "I don't and I'm scared and Uncle Walt can't help and I don't even know where you are."

"I'm on the ground," he said, keeping his own voice soft and smooth, "and you'll be, too, in just a few minutes."

"I'll crash—"

"I won't let you." He swallowed and stared down at Rick. "Now, listen, young lady, I'm going to talk you down, whether you're afraid or not. Got that?"

"I don't like it."

"Just listen to me. You're a little over ninety metres off the ground, you're heading straight for the runway—you know what a runway is, don't you?"

"Yes, but—"

"No *buts* about it. Right now we don't have time

to think. Just do." He hesitated a moment, bent forward, and peered through the plane's windscreen. "I'm watching you all the way. Ease the throttle back another centimetre, hold the wheel right where it is, put both feet on the pedals but don't press either one . . . now . . . ease the wheel forward just a little . . . not too much . . . right, right . . . back on the throttle another centimetre . . . you're looking good, you're looking good."

Mike cupped his hand over the mike and took a deep breath. He realized that the Kadet was wobbling right and left and that the nose was too high. Also, she should have her flaps down, but he was not sure she could handle them. He wiped the back of his hand across his forehead, smearing the perspiration. His throat was dry and he could not keep from squeezing the wheel, even though he knew he must not let his voice betray his own apprehension. He couldn't be sure, but it seemed that her airspeed was too low, that she was right at the point of stalling. Just a little farther, a little farther. He stared hard. And suddenly his hand began to tremble . . .

Rick watched as the Kadet moved nearer and nearer. Gliding, wobbling, turning from side to side, the tail seeming to swish as little gusts of air swept against it. His chin trembled and his hands, rammed deep inside his pockets, knotted into tight fists. "No, no, no—Debbie, don't—don't!"

The plane seemed to swing hard to the right, hesitate, then right itself. But it was too low, too low. And the nose looked like it was going to tilt forward.

"Mike!" Debbie's voice was shrill and panicky.

"Throttle forward, Debbie." Mike's voice was

as low as it had been, as calm and controlled. "More, more, Debbie."

The Kadet seemed to nose forward, as if it would glide right into the ground nose first, and it got lower, lower. Rick shook all over.

"Throttle all the way forward."

Suddenly the sound of the engine changed and the propeller seemed to whir with a shrill cry. Moments before, Rick was certain the plane would slam into the growth of brush between the fence and the runway's end. Instead, the Kadet levelled out and skipped over the earth, not more than fifteen metres off the ground.

"Good girl, good girl," Mike said. He could have been asking somebody what time it was, the words came so gently. "Now—now, ease the wheel towards you—not too much, a little more now."

"What'd I do, what'd I do?"

"You did just fine," Mike said. "But a little crosswind made you swing too much. Didn't you feel it?"

"You're just saying that." Her voice came stuttery and thin. "I almost crashed and know I did." A desperate sob came from Mike's speaker. "I can't land it, I can't, I can't."

"Come on, now—sure you can. I'll just guide you round the field, bring you back to the starting point once more, and this time you'll put it right where you want it."

"No, no, no, no, no!"

"Debbie, Debbie," and for the first time there was a hint of sternness in Mike's voice, "every pilot has to make a pass at the runway sometime or other. I did, Al did, Alice did—everybody does."

"But they can see and I can't."

"All right. But right now ease the wheel back—

that's right, back a little more—too much, steady, steady . . . you've got it." He cupped his hand over the microphone, dabbed at his forehead, and glanced quickly at Hans. "I don't know," he said softly. "I'm afraid she's not going to be able to make it this way."

Rick started to shake. "Mister, you can't just let her crash."

Hans put a hand on Rick's shoulder. "Son, Mike's not going to let that happen. Believe it."

"Did you get a good look at the windscreen?"

The huge hand patted the shoulder. "Yes," he said softly, "I saw it."

"I bet it's cold in that cockpit. And Uncle Walt's probably dead already—"

"He's hurt," Hans said quickly. "But maybe not dead." He turned to Mike. "Are you going to talk her round and down again?"

Mike shook his head. "I don't know, I don't know. If she could just see the runway—" he caught himself and glanced quickly at Rick.

Rick swallowed hard and looked away. He guessed they'd seen the tears in his eyes, but he couldn't help it. They were just people with names, not anybody he'd ever known before, not anybody who really cared about Debbie or Uncle Walt. Sure, they knew how to fly, that man talking to Debbie, maybe he was the best instructor around, maybe he had talked other pilots down when they had trouble. But it was his sister and uncle in that plane and he couldn't help being scared, especially when that man, that Mike said she wasn't going to be able to make it.

"Debbie," Rick turned at the sound and looked once more towards Mike, who was concentrating on the microphone, "ease the throttle back a centimetre—now another centimetre . . . give the wheel a little turn to the left and move it barely forwards . . . hey, good girl, good girl.'' He hesitated a moment, then cleared his throat. ''Al, how's it look?''

''She's in a good climbing pattern, back up to about a hundred and fifty, fifty-five.''

''All right, Debbie—did you hear that? You're climbing just fine.''

''I don't want to climb—I want to get on the ground and get out—I'm freezing!''

''I know, honey,'' Mike said softly. ''But just keep flying till we help you down.''

Hans motioned for Mike to cover the radio mouthpiece. ''Are you going to bring her round again?''

Mike hesitated a moment, then turned toward Rick. ''Son, were you close by when they took off?''

''No, sir—I was at the barn.''

''You don't know, then, how much fuel—''

''Oh, that,'' Rick scratched the side of his neck, wanted to wipe away a tear that had trickled down his cheek but didn't want them to see him do it. ''I heard Uncle Walt tell Charlie—he's a man who works for him—to fuel up.''

Mike glanced toward Hans. ''And what time did she say they left the airstrip?''

''I believe she told Mindy two-o-three.''

Mike made a face, seemed to be making a calculation that Rick didn't understand. ''Three-twenty-five now—that means she has another couple of hours' fuel.'' He turned his attention once more to the microphone, leaning to the side so he could look out of the window in Debbie's direction. ''Debbie, ease the wheel forward—about two centimetres . . . hold it, hold it . . . good—now, Al, how does she look?''

"Beautiful. Levelling off at ninety!"

"Now, Debbie, you'll need to make a turn to the left—remember how to do it?"

"I don't know."

"Tell me what you think you ought to do."

"I—I turn the wheel to the left, hold it back just a little, push on the pedal with my left foot, and count to four."

"Hey, good girl—except this time count to six—and you know what to do when the turn's completed, don't you?"

"I turn the wheel back to the right—back where it was. I push on the right pedal. And maybe ease the wheel forward—is that right?"

"Couldn't do it better if I were right there with you," Mike said. "We're going to make a kind of circle now, and when we finish it, you'll be heading for the runway once more. This time we'll—"

"No!"

"*No*, what?"

"I know I can't do that again. It felt like I was falling, like the front end of the plane was almost pointing straight down. I just can't do it."

Rick took a deep breath and turned so neither Mike nor Hans could see his face. He swallowed back a choking sob, then shaded his eyes with his left hand as he stared into the bright afternoon skies. He'd heard her sound like that before—she was tired of trying, tired of listening to somebody tell her how to do something when she couldn't see. He remembered one day in the summer when he and his father were trying to talk her into diving—she's been a good diver, too, and it wasn't anything really new. She'd reached the end of the board, she'd even raised herself on tiptoe, the way she was supposed to. But then she'd tottered, hadn't been able to keep her balance, and had cried out, "No, no, no!" and had let herself sit limply down on the board's rubber mat.

Mike turned to Hans, shaking his head. "She's too frightened, too frightened. She could come in just right, or she could freeze up and come in—" he caught himself and looked sharply at Rick. "I think we'd better change plans."

"And do what?"

"Birmingham—they've got foam, equipment, everything they need."

"She can't make it there."

"She can make it there just like she made it from Cottonwood to here," Mike said. "Al and Alice can fly with her, give her directions. No question that she's got a pretty good head on her shoulders." Once more he glanced at Rick. "Pretty smart sister you have, son. She can follow Al's directions. They can put her right on the Number Four runway, foam it."

"What about the commercial flights coming in?"

"Divert—the same as for any other emergency. Divert to Atlanta or Huntsville."

"Are you sure?"

"Right now I'm not sure about anything," Mike said softly, "but that kid's going to get so cold up there in a little while she won't be able to think, much less fly."

"All right," Hans said abruptly. He raised the walkie-talkie. "Al?"

"Yeah?"

"One-one-nine-point-five."

Hans deftly turned one of the small dials on the walkie-talkie. "You with me?"

"Roger. What's up?"

One-one-nine-point-five. Rick had never used a radio like the one Hans was talking on but he could guess what was going on. They'd been talking on a different frequency and Hans probably wanted to tell Al something he didn't want Debbie to hear. Rick strained to listen, pretending to be casual but concentrating hard on Hans' words, feeling that whatever was said would have to do with what they'd try now.

"Mike's concerned—says he's afraid the kid won't be able to come in here."

"Any suggestions? You know she hasn't got an endless supply of fuel. And with that windscreen half gone, wind cutting through the cabin—"

"I know, I know," Hans broke in. "But we believe it'd be better to get her to the Birmingham Airport."

"Who's there? Nobody can talk her down better than Mike. You know it, I know it, and Gordie Taylor knows it."

"But we're not equipped here for foam."

"Hans, do you know what you're saying? The pilot's condition, that windscreen, the commercial flights and all."

"We can get the commercials diverted. Ground the private aircraft until the emergency's over."

There was a pause in the communication and Rick found himself shaking all over. Guide her to Birmingham, talk her down, not tell her what they meant for her to do, let her crash into that foamy stuff, maybe get hurt or maybe drown in it. He didn't know what it was, looked like the kind of soap his father used when he shaved. Didn't think Debbie would like that stuff all over her.

Rick didn't like it.

But there was nothing he could do.

"All right," Al was saying, "Let's get to it. What about Alice?"

"She'll fly with you—a little above and back."

"I don't think Mike can talk her all the way."

"He won't try," Hans said. "You'll do it."

There was another long pause. "I'll do what I can," Al finally said. "But, dear God, I feel for that kid."

"So do we all," Hans said. "I'm calling Gordie now."

"Roger."

"And, Al—good luck."

Without waiting for Hans to switch back to Debbie and Mike, Rick eased away from the shadow of the plane's wing, turned, then ran as fast as he could towards the Operations Alcove, where his mother and aunt were waiting. They had to know and he had to tell them because he wasn't certain Mr Mitterwahl would remember to do so . . .

7

Nobody had to tell her. Debbie knew. The nose of the little aircraft had tilted down, too far down. And if Mike hadn't told her what to do and if she hadn't done it immediately, she'd have slammed into the earth. Right there on the runway, or on the ground beside it. And she and Uncle Walt—

She shuddered and shook her head.

But one thing she knew. Whatever else anybody said to her, she was not going to land again. She'd just fly and fly and fly, not even turning, not even moving the wheel or those pedals, not even touching the throttle, and·when the plane ran out of fuel they'd just glide and glide till they hit.

She didn't care.

She was too cold to care, too hurting all over to care, too tired to care. Too blind to care.

"Debbie?"

She sucked air at the corners of her mouth. Her lips felt nearly frozen. "Yes, sir."

"Mike again. We're not going to try bringing you in here. We're going to try something different."

"I'm glad because I don't ever want to do that again. But what else?"

"Al and Alice are going to fly with you—they're going to guide you to Birmingham—"

"I don't want to go to Birmingham!"

"Listen to me," Mike said, his voice still low but once more stern. "They are going to guide you to the Birmingham Airport. We're calling the people up there now. They'll clear out all the big planes and put foam on a runway. Then it won't matter. You can come down into it and it'll be like landing in piles and piles of cotton."

"*I don't want to do that!*"

"I know you don't, honey—and I wish I could do it another way. But it's the best thing now."

Debbie sniffed. She wished she could move her right hand and rub it across her face, wipe away the tears on her cheeks. But she was afraid that if she got her fingers off the wheel rim she'd never make them curl over it again. Once more she sniffed. "Why can't they put foam here?"

"Don't have the equipment—and it'd take too long to get it here." He paused, then added, "Al and Alice will be right there with you. All the way. And I'll be listening."

"I want to come down right now."

"I know you do, honey, and we want you to. But it'll be much safer there—believe me."

Debbie tried to sigh but the best she could do was puff her cheeks and blow air through the corners of her mouth. "How long will it take?"

"Twenty-five, thirty minutes to fly there, another five to line up with the runway, then a few minutes more."

She added the time, came up with something over forty minutes. Nearly an hour. She didn't like it. She squeezed her eyelids shut, forcing the tears out of the corners and down the sides of her nose. The stocking cap felt like it was stuck to her skin. Her hair was matted down her neck, and her ears were so cold she felt that a sudden move would make them break off. She tried to take a deep breath, tried once more to sigh. "I—I guess we have to."

"We have to," Al said simply. "Now, we're heading almost due east—you know which direction that is?"

"I guess if we could just keep flying we'd get to the Atlantic Ocean."

"Roger—except we don't have that far to go. Got your hand on the throttle?"

"Yes, sir."

"Okay. Now easy with the wheel. Turn it gradually to the left. Little more, little more . . . good, good . . . a little push on the left pedal . . . not too much . . . good, you've got it. Now, push the throttle forward about a centimetre, maybe a little more."

Turn the wheel, push the pedal, push the throttle, pull the wheel back, no, go forward with it, no that's too much, and the throttle again, don't forget the throttle. Debbie tried to give her head a little shake and knew that if she ever got on the ground again she wouldn't ever, ever, ever want to fly anymore.

"Beautiful, beautiful," Al said. "We're making a slow climbing turn now. In a minute—don't do anything till I say—in a minute you'll straighten out. Then we just continue climbing."

Climbing, turning, going up, heading—she guessed—north. She knew which way Redfern was from Birmingham—went south most of the way, except when the highway swung east. The road going to Redfern branched to the right.

"How're you doing?"

"I'm freezing and my hands hurt bad."

"But you can still grip the wheel and throttle?"

She wanted to say she couldn't get either hand off the controls. "Yes, sir."

"Good, good. We'll keep going this direction over the mountains and then we'll start dropping down once we get on the other side."

The mountains! She'd forgotten about Double Oak and the Columbia Ridges. Never thought much about them because the highway went around one and through a gulley when it got to the other. And when she'd flown with Uncle Walt they'd been high enough not to think about them— just look down at them. But then they were high, very high.

She did not want to fly over Double Oak Mountain and those Columbia Ridges. She did not want to climb any higher. She wanted, she wanted, she wanted . . .

As he was walking back towards the Operations Alcove, Hans put the call in to Gordie Taylor. "I know about the commercials, the private aircraft. Man, what else can we do?"

"Nothing, nothing," Gordie said. "Mindy's already alerting Atlanta and Huntsville. Flight 917's due in within three minutes. We'll land him, then we'll close off everything else."

"That's a roger. How about the trucks?"

"I won't wait on them. We'll get them on standby at the runway—did you say Number Four?"

"Won't that be best?"

"Negative. Five is open and wider."

"Okay, make it Five. Oh, by the way, Al and

the girl are on frequency one-one-seven-point-nine—"

"Roger. Mindy was talking to her earlier."

"Right." Hans stopped at the door to the Alcove. "Will you talk her in?"

"Negative. Captain Thomasson from the Civil Air Patrol—"

"Lefty Thomasson? Thought he was in Colorado."

"Got transferred back a month or so ago."

"Well, if Mike can't do it, you've got the next best."

"I'll take either one," Gordie said. "By the way, what about the girl's family?"

"They're here," Hans said. "We'll get them up there as soon as we can."

"Roger."

"Good luck," Hans said. He turned off the radio, stood for a moment on the top step, then opened the door and walked inside.

The women were standing at the window looking out, but both turned at the sound of his footsteps. "Will she make it?"

Hans looked from one to the other, not certain which was Debbie's mother and which was her aunt. "She's a mighty plucky little girl, I give her that," he said. "The two pilots flying with her—" he caught himself, glanced toward Rick.

"He told us," Eth said.

"Did he tell you what we're trying to do?"

"Something about foaming a runway but I thought they only did that for huge passenger planes."

"Normally that's true," Hans said. He crossed towards his desk, glancing vaguely at the stock sheet he'd been working on earlier and dismissing it with a hasty nod. "But we believe it'll work for her. The sheriff's chopper—helicopter—is on the pad just beyond the hangar—Sergeant Jeffers of the sheriff's office is on his way. He'll fly you to the Birmingham Airport. Except," and he looked from one to the other, "he can take only two passengers."

Rick coughed and looked up at his mother. "I—I think I'll stay here. You and Aunt Eva go."

Hans recognized at once the unspoken message. The boy did not want to fly. Without letting on, he put a hand on Rick's shoulder. "I'll see to him here—he'll be all right. Might even let him monitor the radio."

"I—I don't know," Eth started to say.

"But, Mum, you've got to be there. Debbie'll need you. And," he turned toward his aunt, "Uncle Walt'll need you."

Five minutes later, Hans stood at the top step to the Alcove once more, with Rick at his side, watching as the helicopter cleared the field and swung in a wide arc as it headed away. Its flashing rotor made a swishing sound, quite different from the noise of the small planes.

"Will they get there in time?"

"Might get there first," Hans said. "Mr Snow may take some extra minutes circling the field. May even have to wait for the foam to be laid down." He stepped down to the concrete walk leading to the hangar. "Might as well tell Mr Griffin that they'll not be back."

"Do you think that my sister will be able—you know—to get the plane on the ground?"

"I'm sure she will this time," Hans said. Words, he thought, knowing that she might do the same thing at the Birmingham Airport that she'd done earlier here. She'd not really panicked, the way some young student pilots occasionally did. But there'd been apprehension, uncertainty. He couldn't blame her—after all, how many trained pilots, skilled ones, would want to bring down any aircraft without being able to see the instruments, the runway, or the field?

Halfway to the place where the parked Kadet was tied down, Hans once more turned on the walkie-talkie.

"Mr Snow?"

"Just call me Al or Snowman, Debbie. What is it?"

"How far are we from the mountains?"

Rick stopped and stared up at Hans. "Does she have to go over old Double Oak?"

"I guess they're taking the most direct route," Hans said. "That would be over Double Oak and the Ridges."

"I don't think Debbie'll like that—won't they have to go lots higher?"

"Some."

"Why couldn't they fly through that gulley or gorge—you know, where the road cuts through?"

"A good pilot can do that," Hans said, "but wind gusts sometimes buffet the planes. Particularly this time of day. It'll be safer over the mountain and ridges."

"Do we have to keep going higher?" Debbie's voice was not as relaxed as it had been earlier.

"Some."

"How much?"

"Oh, not as high as you and your uncle were."

"But how much?"

"She's getting real scared again," Rick said in a soft voice. "I know."

Before Hans could comment, Mike Griffin approached them, paused, and smiled at Rick. "I think we're doing the best thing."

"I hope so," Hans said.

"Wish I could have done better with her. If I could have had about fifteen more minutes with her before we started the approach, we might have pulled it off—"

"Mr Snowman," and now Debbie's voice was breaking, "I'm not going any higher. I don't want to go up any more than this."

Hans stopped suddenly, looked from Rick to Mike.

"What'll she do?" Rick asked.

"But, sweetheart, you won't even know you're climbing," Al said.

"What's she going to do?" Rick repeated, looking first at Hans, then at Mike.

"I can feel it," Debbie said. "When the nose goes up, I feel it."

"But we're well on the way."

"I'm not going."

Hans looked at Rick, then turned to Mike. "Poor kid. Dear God, poor kid . . ."

Debbie felt tightness all over. Her outstretched right arm hurt, her hips were numb, and she knew she would never again be able to unclasp the fingers of her left hand from the knob at the end of the throttle lever. She wanted to go to sleep, to get out of this little plane and away from the controls and out of the wind that was beating and beating her. She wanted to get out and go somewhere and just lie down, just go to sleep and not wake up for a long, long time. This was a nightmare, that's what this was, just a bad, bad nightmare.

If she could just yell for her dad.

Like she did that first night, back in the middle of May, when she woke up to go to the bathroom and couldn't see anything but a blur. She'd stood beside her bed, weaving, almost tottering, staying up only by clutching at a nearby chair. She'd blinked and blinked, then screamed for her dad to come help her.

He came to her room, guided her through the hall, then called her mother to come and help her.

He couldn't come to her now. Neither could her mother. Nor Aunt Eva. Not even Rick—

She screamed and screamed and screamed.

"Debbie!"

She did not answer.

"*Debbie!*" and now Al's voice was stronger, concern evident in its tone. "What's wrong?"

Her body shook and she squeezed the wheel rim tighter than ever. She turned it hard to the right, twisted it back and hard to the left. She kicked the right pedal, then kicked the left one. She pushed the wheel forward, brought it back, pushed the throttle up and back and up and back once more.

"Debbie! Debbie!"

She could not stop crying and as the tears flowed down the sides of her nose, the wind blowing in seemed to freeze them.

"I can't, I can't, I can't do it!"

"Debbie," the voice was controlled and easy. "Debbie," it said again.

She tried to swallow but there was nothing to swallow. Everything inside her was all cried out.

"Debbie," and now it was Al, "easy, easy— you're back on course but you're too low—"

"I'm not going to the Birmingham Airport."

"You have to—"

"I'm not."

"Debbie," and now it was Mike, she could always tell. She supposed that if she turned around and flew right back to the Tri-County Airport and just crashed right in the middle of the runway, he'd still be talking calmly.

"Debbie, what do you want to do?"

"I want to get out of this plane! I'm scared!"

There was a momentary pause, then a different voice came on. "Hey, stupid—I'm the one that's scared of planes. You're not!"

Rick's voice blocked out all other sounds . . .

Mike took the walkie-talkie from Hans and brought it close to his mouth. "Al, turn her around—bring her back this way. If she doesn't want to go to Birmingham, she doesn't have to."

"Now?"

"Now."

Once more there was a pause, then, "Debbie, you heard him. We're going back. Remember, turn the wheel to the left, easy, easy, and push down on the left pedal but not too hard. Hold the wheel a little towards you, good, good—"

Mike handed the walkie-talkie to Hans, spun, and started trotting towards the parked Kadet.

Hans stood for a minute. "What're you going to do?"

"Going up," Mike shouted over his shoulder.

"Wait—I'll move the chocks and ropes!"

As if not knowing what else to do, Rick trotted with them. At the plane, Mike opened the door and started to climb aboard, then paused, "How about fuel—"

"We took care of that this morning," Hans said.

Rick stopped at the door. "What're you going to do, mister?"

"I don't know," Mike said, "but I mean to keep her from crashing." He realized immediately that the word was the wrong one to use. He turned towards Rick. "I won't let your sister get hurt if I can help it. How about it—want to go with me?"

"I'm—I'm afraid to fly."

"Your sister's not," Mike said softly. Then, despite the urgency, he watched the boy's face. "It's hard up there for her—nobody but strangers to talk to, can't see. You know," he chose his words carefully, "sometimes one good, familiar voice is better than all the advice in the world."

Rick stared towards the far end of the runway, stood for a moment with his back half-turned towards Mike. Then slowly he brought himself round to face the man. "Do you think I can help?"

"I know you can."

Rick turned towards Hans, who'd removed the chocks and untied the ropes and was now standing near the wing's tip. "What about my mother and Aunt Eva?"

"We'll get in touch with them—don't worry."

"My mother might not like it if I go up."

"I understand," Mike said, reaching for the door latch. "Hans, I'll pick them up just beyond Three Forks Junction. You might tell Al and Alice to come on down—I'll take over from here," and he started to close the door.

"Wait." Rick took a step closer, hesitated, then deliberately moved to the door's edge. "I'm going, too. She might need me to help her . . ."

8

As Mike taxied the small Kadet across the grass towards the runway, Rick thought about the small garden tractor Uncle Walt used around the barn to haul hay and grain or to cut the lawn between the two stretches of driveway that circled in from the road. The tractor noise was worse, but the sound was quite similar, and he knew the bumps were the same. The difference was that he knew he was not on the tractor. When he'd driven that, he knew just where he was going, knew he wouldn't travel too fast, and knew he could stop, get off, and walk away from it any time.

He couldn't do the same now.

Staring through the windscreen, he could see the blur caused by the propeller and the roof of a small building at the far side of the runway. Beyond, he could make out thick woods. He had to turn and look out the side to see the ground. He sniffed and caught the end of his seat belt, tugging it the way Mike had told him to, drawing it tight. He didn't want to slip around on the seat.

When they reached the runway's end, Mike

turned the plane to a slight angle, revved up the engine, then slipped on his headset. He pointed to the other set, on a hook at the side of the instrument panel. "Put it on."

It was different from the kind Uncle Walt had—this one had only one earpiece and a wider microphone that came round and stuck out about two centimetres from his mouth. He supposed one earphone was better than two. The person in this seat could hear anything the pilot said and could still listen to the radio.

Mike pointed to the instrument panel. "That's the airspeed indicator," he said, directing Rick's attention to a large round dial that looked much like a car speedometer "and that's the altimeter—tells us how high we are." He pointed to a dial on the right. "That's the compass—but you know what a compass is, and that other one, the red and blue ball-like thing inside the glass, that's the turn and bank indicator—tells us whether we're going right, left, or straight."

Rick nodded, but he really didn't care what the instruments were. It didn't matter which said what. All he wanted to do now was get in the air, find Debbie, talk her down, and get out.

"The last one here tells us how much fuel we have—like a car's fuel gauge."

Rick swallowed and stared at three knobs just below the panel.

"That," Mike said, noticing where his attention was, "is the radio."

Again Rick nodded. Just go on, he thought. Just go on and find her and bring her back. I don't think I'm going to like this one little bit.

"Relax," Mike said easily. "You'll like it."

Rick swallowed and once more tugged at the seat belt strap.

Mike revved up the engine once more, eased the plane about, and pushed the throttle forward. "Flight N-2251-Eagle prepared for take-off."

"N-2251-Eagle, you're cleared."

The little Kadet vibrated as Mike released the brakes and permitted the craft to start rolling forwards. At first, Rick thought it didn't feel any different from riding along the road that ran past Uncle Walt's house—that one was sort of bumpy, anyway. But as they gathered speed, as the vibrations increased and the sound of rushing air penetrated the small cabin, he didn't feel at all as if he were riding in a car. He forced himself to slouch down, pressing his body against the seat, and as the sound of the runway suddenly vanished and he realized they were airborne, he reached down and clutched the frame of the seat. When Mike pulled the wheel towards himself and the nose rose more rapidly than he'd expected it to, Rick had to stifle a tight little cry that rose in his throat.

"You okay?"

Rick nodded. But no, I'm not, he thought, I'm not all right and I wish I hadn't said anything about going with you. You don't need me. You're the instructor and I don't know anything about planes.

He stared for a moment through the windscreen and saw nothing but blue, cloud-spattered sky. Then he squeezed his eyes tightly shut.

"Rick, have you ever flown before?"

"Once. Three years ago we flew to Atlanta, then to Washington. Wasn't bad going to Atlanta but the little plane we rode from there to Washington got caught in a storm—lightning and rain and everything—felt like we were going to be knocked down. I couldn't help it—I cried." He took a deep breath. "My mother came back with me on the train."

"Storms don't often knock aircraft out of the sky," Mike said.

The Kadet rolled gently to the right, steadied briefly, then banked again to the right, this time more sharply. Rick felt himself sliding and grabbed wildly for the seat's edge with his free hand. "I don't like it," he said.

Mike levelled off. "Just try to relax—how about it?"

"I'm—I'm trying."

"Take a deep breath and let it out slowly."

Rick breathed in until he couldn't suck in any more, puffed out his cheeks, and blew.

"Not that way—like this," and Mike inhaled slowly.

Rick partially opened one eye and glanced at him. The Kadet sailed steadily, and beyond Mike, through the window, he saw the clouds once more. Gradually, he forced himself to open both eyes. "Are you going to turn again?"

"Not that sharply," Mike said. "We're heading for Three Forks Junction now." He turned on the radio, looked at the dial, nodded to himself, and twisted the knob with one quick motion.

"When's he coming?"

That was Debbie's voice and Rick momentarily forgot where he was. "She's talking about you."

Mike nodded. "Be right with you, Debbie," he said into the microphone.

Rick turned to him. "How're you going to talk her down?"

Mike looked straight at him "I wasn't sure until you decided to come with me—but this time I'm going to teach you how to fly."

"Huh? I don't want to—"

Mike covered the mouthpiece. "We'll tell her you're with me, that I'm telling you how to handle the controls—and I want her to do everything you do, when I say do it."

"That doesn't make sense. Besides, all I want is to get her down safely. I'm not ever going up in another plane."

"You want to help, don't you?"

"Yes," he said slowly.

"Okay—if she knows you're with me, if she hears me telling you what to do, she'll be thinking about it—get her mind off the tight spot she's in."

Rick thought for a moment. A kind of game, that's what it was. Like once when he didn't want to learn how to play dominoes and Dad wanted him to learn. So—he taught Debbie. "It won't work." But with the dominoes it had worked for him. After his dad had gone to the study, he'd played three games with Debbie. Beat her the last one.

"Let's tell ourselves it *will* work," Mike said. "Are you going to help?"

Rick made a face and stared straight ahead. One thing he knew for certain—he was never again going to get in anybody's plane. He also knew one other thing—he did not want his sister to go crashing down in that Kadet and get herself—

He choked back the thought.

"I'll—I'll try."

"Good boy." Mike reached across and patted his knee. Then he glanced to his left and suddenly pointed in that direction. "Over there—there they are."

Forgetting that he was belted to the seat, Rick sat forward and strained to see over Mike's shoulder. There they were, all three of them—the red and white Kadet with its broken windscreen, a shiny silver-looking plane that was a little bigger than Debbie's, and a green one that looked like it had a low wing. "Debbie, Al, and Alice, I have you in sight."

"Roger," Al said.

"She's doing fine, just fine," Alice said. Rick didn't know for sure, but Alice sounded like she was trying to keep her voice cheerful. He guessed that was what she thought she ought to do.

"I can tell," Mike said. "Now, Debbie, Al and Alice are going to leave us and I'll take over. Okay?"

"Okay—I guess."

"That'll just leave the four of us up here."

"Four?"

"Debbie, pull the wheel back just a bit—hey, that's it," Mike said. "Yes, four—you, your uncle, me, and a student."

"Student? You're not teaching somebody else—how, with me here?"

"He's got something to say to you," and Mike nodded at Rick.

Rick touched his tongue to his lips and turned his eyes towards Mike. "Debbie—it's me. Rick."

"Huh?" There was a pause. "Rick? Rick, is that you? What're you doing in a plane?"

"Mike—Mr Griffin's going to teach me how to fly."

"But why? You don't like flying—"

"Debbie," Mike broke in, "Rick's along because he wants to help you." He glanced at the boy briefly. "I can't really teach you or him how to fly in the little time we have. But I told him I'd teach both of you something—right now, how to land an aircraft."

"How can you do that if he's—"

"Debbie," Mike interrupted her, "ease the throttle forward—that's good, and pull the wheel back just a little. Good, good."

"But how can you teach us both?"

"Simple," Mike said. "I'll tell Rick what to do and watch him do it. Everything I tell him, I want you to do, too. And, Debbie, if he thinks I'm not telling you right, he'll say so."

"Ha!" and for the first time since he'd been listening to her, Rick thought he detected a natural sound in her voice. "How will he know?"

"I guess he knows you pretty well. I guess you've played games together and gone places. Maybe he can describe something for you—we'll just have to see."

"Rick, aren't you scared?"

"Yeah."

"Me, too—scareder than I've ever been."

"I know," Rick said quietly. "And that's why I'm here."

"First," Mike said, "we're not going back to the airport—at least, not now. We're going to fly over a huge farm, lots of flat land about three minutes from where we are now. When we reach it, I'll start telling Rick what to do. You listen carefully, Debbie. Do what he does—and I'll be watching both of you."

"It doesn't make sense," Debbie said.

"Well, just do it," Rick said.

Mike nodded and smiled. Cupping his hand over the mouthpiece, he leaned towards Rick. "Put your right hand there, on the rim of the wheel. Grip it but don't squeeze it. Now, put your left hand there," he pointed to the knob at the end of the throttle lever, "and hold it the same way."

"Is that what she's doing?"

"We told her that already." Mike pointed down. "Stretch your legs and put your feet on those pedals. Good. Now," he took his own hands off the controls, "you're flying."

"Hey, hey, I can't."

"But you're doing it. Just hold on. Debbie," he said into the mouthpiece, "Rick's flying, same as you."

Rick swallowed and felt his throat drying out. "I don't think I like it."

"You're doing fine, just fine." Mike glanced off to his left. "Debbie, before we get there, take your hand off the wheel and flex your fingers."

"I can't. They're stuck."

"Well, try working the fingers, anyway. And do the same with the left hand." Once more he covered the microphone and turned back to Rick. "See that lever in front of the throttle?"

Rick glanced furtively down, not knowing whether the plane would remain on course unless he kept his eyes straight ahead. "Yes."

"It controls the flaps—anybody ever tell you what flaps were?"

Rick shook his head.

"Okay, then, we'll have to believe Debbie doesn't know about them, either."

"Can't we just go ahead and find out about landing so we can get her down?"

"That's what flaps are for," Mike said. "They help you land."

"But it takes three hands if you have to do something with that stick."

"You use the same one that's holding the throttle." Mike removed the hand that was over the microphone and nodded to Rick. "All right, Rick" he said loud enough so that his voice was transmitted, "right there on your left, just ahead of the throttle, there's a control lever—do you see it?"

Trying to follow the instructions and relay them too, Rick nodded. "You mean that black rod that looks like a short poker? About twenty centimetres in front of the throttle?"

Mike nodded a *good, good* signal. "That's right. Now, don't look at it but ease your hand from the throttle knob to the end of the other one."

Lowering his shoulder, Rick bent to the left, closed his eyes as if pretending he were blind, and moved his hand forward until his fingers came in contact with the lever. "Don't know how many centimetres it is but it's about as far as from the edge of the doorway in Debbie's room to the light switch." He glanced quickly at Mike.

Mike nodded *good, good.*

"I—I think I've found it," Debbie said. "What does it feel like?"

"You know those little grass clippers Mum got two summers ago—when you were going to trim the edge of the lawn but you never did?"

"I know, I know," Debbie said. "Do you hold it or squeeze it?" Rick looked quickly to Mike.

Mike broke in. "When you pull it up, you don't squeeze it, but when you let it down, you do."

"What's it for?"

"It controls the flaps," Mike said. "You don't use flaps to fly, but when you want to land, the flaps help slow your speed and increase the angle—" he caught himself, "they help you go down more quickly without gaining speed." He touched Rick's hand, indicating for him to move his fingers from the flap control. "You'll have to use them, so right now we'll apply them just a little—sort of feel what they do. But not much." He tapped Rick's hand, signalling for him to pull the lever.

"How much?"

Mike spread his thumb and forefinger apart about two centimetres. "Ready, Debbie?"

"I—I guess so."

"About as far as from the edge of the table to the edge of your plate."

"Good boy," Mike whispered, then glanced left toward the Kadet Debbie was flying. "Now," he said, "pull easy."

Even though he'd moved it no more than Mike said, Rick felt the sudden bump, as if the plane had been jolted. He trembled and turned quickly to Mike. "What happened? Did I do wrong?"

"Mike!" Debbie's voice was tight and strained. "Something happened!"

"It was supposed to make that bump," Mike said gently. "It wasn't much, but it slowed down the plane," and he pointed to the airspeed indicator so Rick could see.

Rick swallowed and took a deep breath. He put his hand over the microphone. "I don't like it—I don't like it a bit."

"You're doing fine, just fine," Mike whispered. "Now," he said aloud. "squeeze the lever and push it back down—squeeze hard, though, before you try to push."

Rick followed the directions and once more he felt the plane tremble. This time, however, he was expecting it. "Hey, that was easy."

"Easy for you," Debbie said, "but I'm getting colder and colder—can't we just go ahead?"

"We're going ahead soon." Mike said. "Debbie, right now we're flying at three hundred metres. Do you know what that means?"

"We're three hundred metres off the ground."

"Right. And we're coming up on that field I was telling you about. So listen carefully. I'm going to tell Rick what to do and you can hear me. If he thinks he can tell you something to make it easier, he'll interrupt. Okay?"

"Are we going to land now—I mean, try to?"

"Not really. But we're going to learn how to. We'll pretend we're just a hundred metres—"

"I thought you said we were three hundred metres up?"

"I did—we're just going to pretend we're a hundred metres off the ground. That's how high you'll be when you really start down. When I say *flaps*, you pull that lever up. When I say *throttle back*, you pull the throttle knob. And when I say *wheel forward* or *wheel back*, that's what I want you to do. But both of you remember this—keep even pressure on both pedals." He glanced at Rick, got a hesitant nod, then said, "Now—flaps."

When the flaps went down and the two planes bucked at the sudden change of speed, both Rick and Debbie screamed . . .

9

As soon as the small helicopter landed, Eth and Ev scrambled out of it and hurried to the door of the Operations Alcove. Without knocking, they barged in and crossed to the desk where Hans was monitoring the walkie-talkie. "What's the matter—what happened to Debbie?"

Hastily Hans switched off the radio and stood up. "Mrs Whitfield, Mrs Hodges—nothing's happened."

"I thought Debbie was going to the Birmingham Airport—that foam stuff—"

"She wouldn't go."

"What do you mean, wouldn't go?"

He glanced from one to the other. "I think she became frightened when they told her she'd have to go over the mountains."

"Oh, dear God," and Eth clutched her sister's arm. "And she's out there not knowing what to do . . ."

Hans hurried around the edge of the desk and caught both women by their elbows. "She's all right," he said softly.

"But where is she, what's she doing? Isn't anyone doing anything to help her? Dear God," and Eth put her hand up to her face, "my child's going to crash that plane—"

"Eth, Eth," Ev said, "they're doing the best they can." She looked at Hans. "Did she say anything—has she even mentioned her uncle?"

"Once. All she said was that he hadn't moved, hadn't spoken to her. But, you know, not being able to see—she can't be sure."

"But what about her now?" Eth choked back a tight sob.

"Mike's up with her—"

"How?"

Hans explained about the two planes, about what Mike had in mind. "He'll not try to teach her anymore than he has to, and as soon as he thinks she can follow landing directions, he'll bring her down."

Eth shuddered, glanced toward the huge window. "Where's Rick?"

Hans took a deep breath. "He's with Mike—"

"Flying? But he can't. He's deathly afraid of flying. Why did that man take my son—"

"Rick wanted to go."

"He couldn't want to fly."

"No, I guess he didn't," Hans said slowly. "But he said something about helping his sister. That probably outweighed his fear."

Eth turned, put her hand on Ev's shoulder. "My children—I don't think I can take it—"

"Eth, it's going to be all right. That Mr Griffin—" she glanced at Hans.

"Mike Griffin," he said.

"He's a good pilot—"

"Probably the best pilot to fly out of this airfield since I've been here," Hans said. "And he won't give up." He guided them across the room towards the couch and was suggesting that they sit down when the door popped open and Alice walked in.

They turned quickly.

"Alice," Hans said, "Mrs Whitfield and Mrs Hodges." He nodded toward Eth. "Debbie's mother. Alice Curwitz—she's been flying with them—was going to Birmingham."

Alice nodded, tried to smile. "That's a courageous young girl you have, Mrs Whitfield."

Eth dabbed at her eyes. "Was she making sense when she decided to turn around?"

"For a moment," Alice said, "we weren't sure. But believe me, she knew exactly what she wanted to do. And not do."

"You were close to her plane, did you say?" Ev asked.

"Close enough to see in the cabin."

"My husband?"

"I could only make out a form. He was leaning back, but that's all I could tell."

"He didn't move?"

"I was too far away to tell," Alice said. She turned to Hans. "That duck or goose or whatever really slammed a hole in the windscreen.

"Is the whole windscreen gone, could you tell?"

"No. More like a big hole on the pilot's side." She crossed the room to her desk, sat down, then turned towards Hans. "Mike said he was going to do practice landings over the Southland Farms."

"Practice landings?" Ev looked from one to the other. "I'm no pilot, but how can you do practice landings that way?"

"Oh," Alice said hastily, "they won't actually land—can't. I think he means they'll go to a certain altitude, then follow landing procedures. Let her get the feel of the aircraft. But," and now she turned to Hans once more, "I hate to say it, but how much flying time does she have left?"

"Maybe forty minutes," and Hans glanced at his walkie-talkie. "Can't spend much time working at it."

"And they'll try the final here?"

"Have to," Hans said. He looked over at Eth and Ev. "Mrs Whitfield, Mrs Hodges, Mike's the best. But given the circumstances, I think we'll alert the fire department and the ambulance."

Eth bit her lower lip and glanced from him to her sister. "I—I know," she said softly. "Whatever you have to do."

"I need to turn on the radio. You may not want to listen."

The sisters looked at each other. After a moment, Ev said, "You have to. If we can't, we'll just go outside."

Hans nodded and turned on the walkie-talkie.

All four heard Debbie and Rick scream . . .

10

Debbie could not stop the trembling that shook her whole body. Her hand slipped from the flap lever and flailed about as she reached for the throttle knob. The wheel vibrated, she thought she detected a strange sound coming from the motor, and the wind seemed to be coming in thick gusts. "I'm falling!"

"No, Debbie—no, you're not falling. Just slowing down. Like putting on the brakes of a car, except that the air doesn't have a paved surface."

"I don't like it and I can't find the knob to the throttle."

"Put your hand on your knee," Mike said, "then let it just fall limply."

Her arm jerked spasmodically as she forced the palm of her left hand to press against the side of her thigh, as her groping fingers stretched forward and as the hand crept towards the kneecap. "I can't find it."

"It's—it's about as far from your knee," Rick's voice was breaking, "as Dad's big chair is from the little table."

Debbie thought for a minute and wished she could remember how that charter pilot, what was his name? Jeff?—how Jeff told her to find it. Something about letting her hand just fall, except now she couldn't make the elbow loosen at all. Had to force it. The chair to the table. Her hand kept sinking until her little finger came in contact with the side of the knob. Very carefully, she eased it about until all four fingers were cupping it.

"How about it, Debbie?" Mike's voice, she thought, was no more excited than if he'd been telling her she had a little smudge of soot on her cheek.

"I—I think so."

"Think?"

"I've got it."

"Good, good. Now—we're still at the same altitude—just as high up as we were. But we're flying a little slower. I want you to pull the knob back but not too far."

"How far's not too far?"

"About from the top of your coffee cup to the saucer," Rick said, and this time she noticed that his voice squeaked a little but it wasn't breaking, the way it had moments earlier.

"Good girl," Mike said. "Now ease the wheel forward—don't turn it, keep it straight. But forward."

Debbie moved it slowly, not even a centimetre, stopped, then moved it once more.

"I moved this one about as far as the hot water knob is from the cold one on our bath."

Debbie felt the distance, stopped. "Like that?"

"Maybe a centimetre more," Mike said.

She made the correction. "Now?"

"Couldn't do it better if I were right there beside you," Mike said. "Now, we're going down slowly, just like we'd be doing if we were actually heading for the end of the runway. Nose is down, the air brakes are working, and we're losing speed."

Debbie remembered that Uncle Walt had some kind of red line on that thing called an airspeed indicator—she'd seen it way last year when he'd taken her to Birmingham and back. He'd said there was something called a critical speed. Below it, the nose could drop and the aircraft would spin. "I— I don't want to nosedive." She guessed that was the right word.

"You're not going into a nosedive," Mike said. "But we're dropping down, dropping down. We've come down thirty metres—wait, wait, another fifteen—another fifteen."

"We're getting too close to the ground—"

"No—we're still way up, Now, Debbie, are your feet on the pedals?"

"Yes."

"All right. Now, the brakes are at the upper half of them. Press with the front of your feet for just a moment."

"What'll happen?" She tensed, remembering the flaps.

"Nothing, nothing at all. They're for on the ground—I just want you to know where they are."

She hesitated for a moment, then lightly applied pressure with her toes. "Nothing happens."

"Debbie," Rick's voice was almost normal, "It's sort of like the pedals on your old bicycle except it doesn't go all the way round. Maybe like it's bending a little."

"Wait—wait. I got it—but it doesn't go down much."

"That's right," Mike said. "We're down to two hundred and twenty metres, seventeen, fifteen— Debbie if we were over the runway now, we'd just be six metres off the ground. You could almost fall that far and not get hurt."

"I don't want to fall anywhere. Please!"

"I'm not going to let you," Mike said. "We're right at two hundred and ten—now, we're there. Gradually push the throttle forward and hold the wheel just a little bit towards you—not too much now, easy, easy—"

"Like how far you push the toaster button down to make it work."

"Ours or Aunt Eva's?"

"Ours, stupid—you know we don't make our own toast at Aunt Eva's."

"I did once."

"Well, I never have and I don't know how far that is," Rick said. His voice now was more like his own.

"The speed's picking up," Mike said. "Now, Debbie, Rick, take your hands from the throttle, find the end of the flap control and gently squeeze it. Okay? Now push it down."

"Hey, hey!"

Debbie didn't know what Rick's exclamation meant, but whatever he meant to convey didn't come through as any hey-hey matter. She moved her hand, fumbled for the flap control, nestled her fingers about it, and squeezed. The pressure of air on the flaps made them rise abruptly and she felt the lever almost jerk from her hand. "Oh—oh."

"Debbie?" She didn't know how a man could always keep his voice so calm.

"Yes?"

"Did you feel that?"

"Felt two things—the handle almost popped out of my hand, and the plane felt like it was going to shake to pieces. I don't think I like it."

"You're doing just fine," Mike said. "Now, we'll

climb to three hundred metres, level off, and go through the landing once more."

"Did we do everything we have to, to land?"

"Everything but two—the brakes and the ignition. You have to apply the foot brakes the way I told you, and you have to turn off the ignition switch."

"I—I don't even know where it is."

"It's on the instrument panel—you just lean forward and it's a kind of handle-like thing, except it's not as big."

Debbie leaned forward, slowly took her hand from the throttle, and began to feel her way along the instrument panel. "I can't find it."

There was a brief pause, then Rick said, "It's like you were sitting on the toilet in our bathroom at home and reached for the paper."

"Rick!"

"Well, it is. Try it."

Once more she stretched out her arm, her fingers feeling along the panel. "I think I've found it. Does it feel like the storm door latch—you know, the one that leads to the verandah at home?"

"Hey, yeah—bet it could be used for it."

"Good girl," Mike said. "But, Debbie, do not turn it until I give you the signal. Understand?"

"Yes."

"Fine. Now, pull the wheel back a little more and push the throttle forward. We'll try 'landing' again."

Ten minutes later, as they were levelling off after a second simulated approach to the runway, Debbie tried to shake her hand. But she'd been in the cold too long. Her shoulder ached, her elbow did not want to bend properly, and she had a momentary fear that she'd not be able to handle the throttle, the flaps, and the switch when the time came to do so.

She took a deep breath, wishing the windscreen would magically close, and thought about the steps involved in landing. Mike would guide her till she was heading towards the strip—that she knew. But even though he'd keep telling her what to do, she had to do everything herself. She frowned, wishing again that the stocking cap was not pulled so tightly across her head.

She tried, but try as she might, she could not decide how long she'd been in the air, how long it had been since the goose had flown through the windscreen and hurt Uncle Walt. But one thing she knew. After a certain amount of time the fuel would be gone.

She sniffed and wished she could rub her hand across her nose. Couldn't though. Couldn't do anything but hold the wheel and the throttle and the flap lever, keep her feet on the pedals and fly, fly fly fly.

She gave her head a little shake, clenched her teeth, sensed their momentary chattering, and shuddered. "Mr Griffin—"

"Mike—just Mike."

"I don't want to do any more practice landings."

"We have time—"

"I'm too tired. Too cold. I," and she supposed her sigh was audible through the microphone, "I guess I'm ready to try it."

There was a brief pause. "Are you sure?"

"I'm not sure of anything except that I want to get out of here. And I have to try landing, don't I?"

"Yes, Debbie."

"Okay. But, Mike—please don't let me die . . ."

11

When those words came crisp and clear through the radio monitor in the Operations Alcove of the Tri-County Airport, Eth shuddered and got to her feet. Her gaze went immediately to Hans, now sitting on the corner of his desk, walkie-talkie in hand. "Does that mean they're coming? Now?"

Hans nodded and brought the walkie-talkie close to his face. He turned the small frequency knob. "Lonnie!"

"Yes, sir—right here."

"Where are the fire engines and the rescue vehicle?"

"At the east gate, a little south of the runway."

"You're sure they're clear of it—she may not hit it."

"They're out of the way—got the motors running in case."

"Good, good—and where are you?"

"Just outside the hangar, right by the service truck."

"Right." Hans paused, glanced towards Eth and Ev, then looked away. "The girl's ready to give it a try—and this time there won't be another shot at it. The minute she gets close to the runway, take out after her. She may flip over, cartwheel, nose in—just be there as fast as you can."

"Roger."

Eth stopped at the desk. "Can we do anything? *Anything?*"

Hans shook his head, then glanced toward the window. "Pray."

"We've been doing that," she said quietly.

"Alice?"

"Yes?"

"Call Gordie Taylor. They may be monitoring and may want to send some people down here."

Eth understood what "some people" meant. No matter where it happened, any time a crash occurred, teams of investigators came to look at the debris, study the pieces, recreate the accident, and explain its cause.

She turned about and walked slowly back to where Ev was sitting. "I'm afraid for her."

"If Walt would just come to—I know he's just knocked out."

"But we can't count on that."

"Mrs Whitfield, Mrs Hodges," Hans came across towards them, "I think it'll be a good idea to turn off the monitor."

"We want to know," Eth started.

Ev caught her hand. "He's right."

Eth moved to the end of the battered couch and slowly let herself down on its cool, crinkled cushion. All morning she'd busied herself in Ev's kitchen, making pies, washing dishes, even scouring a pan—to keep her mind off Monday and the operation that Debbie was to undergo. Didn't want to think about what the doctor might or might not be able to do.

Right now, if she could just know they would go to the hospital on schedule, she'd be glad to have that worry.

Ev touched her sister's hand gently. "She'll make it—they'll make it," she said softly. "You heard her. And you've often told me once she makes up her mind to do something, she does it."

"When she can," Eth said. "But this—"

"She can do this," Ev said. "Believe it."

Hans moved from the desk to a wall map, then turned and hurried across the room towards the door. "They'll need me," he said . . .

As he watched Mike work the controls, turning the plane and heading towards Tri-County Airport, Rick guessed that he wasn't as frightened now as he thought he would be. That didn't mean he really liked flying, that this one little ride made him want to become a commerical pilot. But once he got accustomed to the small air bumps, once he saw how the controls worked and understood how simple it was to stay in the air—if you were careful— he didn't know, but maybe he'd like to go up again sometime with Mike. The way he handled the wheel and throttle and pedals, it was as smooth as when his dad put the car on those winding mountain roads he sometimes used on weekends when he wanted to get away from the main highways.

Of course, there was one big difference between driving a car and flying a plane—when you got ready to stop in a car, you just stopped. Couldn't do that with a plane.

As the small craft banked slightly to the right, then turned more sharply to the left, Rick tried to let his body sway with the motion, not fighting it the way he had earlier. It wasn't really like riding in the car—or, for that matter, like anything else he could recall. But it was kind of fun, swinging in the air. He glanced at Mike as the pilot gave Debbie instructions, wishing he already knew how to do what she was being told. Mike gave him a quick nod, then indicated with a flick of his hand that he wanted Rick to put his hand on the wheel and throttle.

"Are we getting close?"

Mike nodded and pointed at the altimeter. As he stared at the indicator and tried to convert the numbers to metres, he realized that as they had flown from the practice area, they had also been losing altitude. Now they were just a little over a hundred and twenty metres up. He turned and stared out the window and was startled to realize how clear and sharp the car outlines were—except they weren't just outlines now. He could make out shapes and sizes and one time he thought he was sure the blue car going along the blacktop road was a Ford.

". . . Now, Debbie, we're lining up with the runway—"

"Both of us?"

"Both," Mike said, "except I'll be to your right."

"Can we land side by side?"

Mike adjusted the small wire-like bracket holding the microphone in place. "No. We'll stay behind so I can watch every move you make."

"Are we close?"

"Very close," Mike said.

Rick shifted his attention and stared through the windscreen. The small plane shuddered once, levelled off, then seemed to rise and fall. Once more Rick turned his attention to Mike's hands, which were deftly working the controls.

"Mike?"

"Yes, Debbie."

"I can't."

"What?"

"I can't do it." There was a pause and Rick looked out the left window, wishing he could see the crippled Kadet, could see through and into the cockpit where she was. But he could not.

"You can do it."

"No, I can't, either, and I know I'll just crash and kill Uncle Walt and myself. And I don't want to die—"

"Debbie! Listen to me. We're running out of time. Find the flap lever."

"W—where—oh, that long handle-like thing."

"Right."

"I—I've got it."

Mike glanced at Rick, nodding toward the control. Rick swallowed and shifted his hand from the throttle to the lever.

"Now pull it up."

Rick pressed the release button and pulled hard as he could. "How far?" he asked.

"All the way. Pull it all the way, Debbie."

"Oh—oh!" Debbie's voice sounded like a little cry.

Rick felt the aircraft vibrate and shudder as the flaps forced the nose downward. "Hey," he said, "is that all right?" He glanced toward Mike and got a responding vigorous nod.

"Fine, just fine."

"I don't like it," Debbie said. "What's happening?"

"We're going down."

"Not too fast—"

"Just right," Mike broke in.

Rick closed his eyes, trying to concentrate on the controls. But just then Mike touched his shoulder. He opened his eyes, stared in the direction Mike was pointing, and spotted what appeared to be a path well to the right of the runway. "We'll land there," Mike said.

Rick's gaze swept the area. "But it's not a real runway—"

"A little plane like this one can land there safely." Mike guided Rick's hand from the flap lever to the throttle. "Time to slow the speed."

Rick closed his eyes.

"Debbie, Rick, pull the throttle back."

"How far?"

Rick felt the distance. "The sugar bowl to the salt shaker."

There was a brief pause, then Mike said, "Okay, you're both doing fine."

Rick swallowed, opened one eye just a bit to see Mike's face, then quickly shut it.

"Now—pull the wheel back."

Rick followed the command, realizing as he did that Mike's hand was on his, guiding it.

"How far?" he heard Debbie ask.

Rick sniffed hard. "The—the toothbrush holder to the drinking glass rack."

Mike turned to stare off in Debbie's direction. "Hey, perfect. Perfect."

Rick felt his heart thumping. At that moment the right wing seemed to dip suddenly and he clutched the wheel. "Hey—"

"What's wrong?" Debbie asked quickly. "What is it?"

Rick swallowed and wished the thumping would stop. "Nothing."

Once more Mike touched his shoulder, and this time when he looked out he could make out more than the ground. Well beyond the end of the field he could see another plane parked to the side, a pickup truck over near one of the buildings, some people bunched up close to a row of parked cars, and two fire engines. And an ambulance.

He couldn't tell how high they were but he knew they were awfully close to the ground because he began to have the sensation of speed, as if he were in a car on a smooth road—

Mike suddenly tapped Rick's arm. "Put your feet on the pedals firmly. And remember what I said about the brakes."

Rick thought hard. "At the top of the pedals? Push with the toes?"

"What'd you say?" Debbie asked.

"I said put your feet on the pedals," Mike said. "But don't push the brakes till I say."

The ground was right under them now, so close that Rick thought he could almost see clumps of weeds. Once more he felt pressure on his left hand.

"Throttle back," Mike said.

"How far?"

But before Mike could answer him, he felt the throttle come to an abrupt stop.

"All the way," Mike said.

"The motor will stop!" Debbie yelled.

"Won't either," Rick said before Mike had a chance. "*Just do it!*"

"*But I don't want to crash!*"

Rick opened his eyes and quickly turned to look past Mike in the direction of Uncle Walt's little Kadet. He could see nothing though.

Debbie fought against the sobs as she pulled back the knob. She struggled to hold the wheel steady as she worked her feet onto the pedals the way Mike had told her to do earlier—so the front of her shoes were ready to press the brakes. She had done everything they'd told her to do—she'd turned, she'd pulled the wheel back, she'd yanked the flap control as far as it would go, and she'd jerked the throttle back.

A tremble passed through her as she listened to the engine. Its sound was distinctly different now, no longer part of the rush and roar of wind through the shattered windscreen. Perhaps the engine had died altogether. Perhaps she was close to the runway. Perhaps she was going to crash—she didn't know.

But there was one thing she did know, one thing she was absolutely positive of. Whatever happened now, she would not make another banking turn. She would not push the throttle forward and climb into the sky once more. This time she was going to touch the ground. This time she was going to do no more than hold onto the wheel.

She tried to fight back the shivers that racked her body but could do no more than tense herself. Numbness had given way to a searing, burning sensation around her face, along both arms, and through her fingers. Her ears felt like weights being held to her head by the pressure of the stocking cap—

"Debbie, pull the wheel back." Mike's voice was as calm as if he were saying to turn off a light switch.

"Hot water knob to cold water knob!" Rick added.

Debbie stopped thinking and responded.

And now there was a different feel, as if the nose of the Kadet had lifted and the air was no longer smooth but becoming mushy, vaguely reminding her of when she floated on a raft off the coast of Panama City Beach—except that the air waves came much faster than the waves on the Gulf. And on the water, she didn't have the sensation of going down, going down—

"Take your hand off the throttle," Mike broke in, "and find the ignition switch."

"What—"

"On the instrument panel," Mike said.

Debbie reached forward, bumped the hard surface with her gloved hand, fumbled around right and left. "Where is it?"

"In the middle. Where you found it before."

"You know," Rick added, "the thing that's shaped like the storm door handle."

She shook all over and was about to yell into the microphone that she couldn't locate it when her frantic fingers contacted the large knob with the handle-like middle. "Do I turn it—"

The words abruptly ended in a shrill cry when the Kadet struck something hard, bouncing her up, slamming her down, then up once more.

"Pull the wheel back, Debbie! Hard! And hold it!"

She pulled it as hard as she could.

Another bump, and another and another. The little plane teetered right and left and right again, vibrated, then tried to pivot to the left.

"Right pedal—right pedal! With your toe! Your toe!"

The wheel seemed to be jerking back and forth, as if some force she could not comprehend was controlling it. She clung to it as hard as she could, the fingers of her right hand locked about the cold rim, her shoulder vibrating with every bounce. She pushed down with the right foot, forcing her ankle to bend so the toe of her shoe applied pressure at the top of the pedal. The Kadet shuddered, tried to cartwheel back to the right, trembled, then tilted to the left as her body swung in one direction, then toppled back in the other direction, towards Uncle Walt.

"Help me!"

Something shattered outside and she just knew the end of the wing was being torn off. She felt herself being swung about, almost being slammed against the right side of the cockpit.

"Turn the switch, Debbie. *Now!*"

Without thinking, she tried to force the switch to the right, found that it would not move, and jerked it the other way. Her fingers felt the firm click and almost at once the engine sputtered, coughed, seemed to catch again, then died like a car out of fuel. The swishing sound of the propeller became a final sigh.

Then nothing.

No wind, no motion, not even a faint vibration.

Slowly, Debbie let her hand slip from the wheel, relaxed both arms, and slumped forward. Violent trembling shook her body, tears came to her eyes and slid down the sides of her nose, her lips worked, and the tightness that had controlled her body seemed to disappear.

"You did it—you did it!" Rick's voice came through the earphones like a distant shout. *"You really did it!"*

Then she heard other sounds—the whine of an ambulance siren, the roar of motors, the skidding of wheels on the runway. And voices—". . . Get the fire extinguisher . . ." and ". . . Open the door on the other side . . ." and ". . . Which side's she on?" and ". . . Better brace that wing . . ."

She sensed the side of the plane next to her being touched by strong, firm hands, the little door being jerked open, someone reaching through and unfastening her safety belt, and gentle arms grasping her.

"Down," she whispered. "Down, down, down. . ."

12

Debbie felt herself being lowered slowly onto a stretcher, and though she could not see them, she knew at least four people were holding her.

"Are you hurt anywhere?"

"—I don't think so. But my fingers and knees and feet ache."

"Cold?"

"Numb."

They pulled a heavy blanket over her and she felt her gloves being carefully removed. When her fingers were free, she tried working them into fists, then stretching them as straight as she could. The effort sent needle-like pain into both wrists. Gingerly, she stretched her feet out, extending her legs, forcing her knees to straighten. Again there were sharp pains.

Someone bent over her and she felt gentle fingers turning up the stocking cap and easing the ribbed turtle-neck down, exposing her face. "Ouch," she said.

"Chapped," a man's voice said. "We'll put something on it."

"Uncle Walt—what about him?"

"Still unconscious. That goose hit him in the chest and stomach, doubled him over and made him crack his head on the wheel."

"Will he—" she caught herself, not wanting to put the thought into a spoken word.

"He's hurt pretty bad but the doctor's with him now. Good thing you got him down when you did."

All kinds of smells were in the air and she tried to distinguish them. She could only be sure of fuel odours, however, and whatever the blanket had been wrapped in. She took a deep breath and tried to swallow.

"Honey, here's some water—"

"Hey—you did it! You did it!"

Rick's voice cut through all the other sounds, and she felt him bump the side of the stretcher as he bent close and grabbed her arm. "You really did it!"

Debbie half turned, reached out, and grabbed him about the neck, pulling him close. "I couldn't have if you hadn't helped."

"I didn't do anything—"

"Yes, he did," a different voice said.

She recognized it. Extending her other hand, she felt for Mike's fingers, gripped them, and pulled him towards her. She knew that he, too, was squatting down beside her. "I guess I would have crashed if you hadn't—if you hadn't," but she couldn't finish.

Mike's hand was warm and tender on her forehead. "Honey, all I did was give directions. You flew it down. You landed it."

"I couldn't have unless somebody told me how." She covered his hand with hers, then turned her face towards him. Slowly she extended one hand upwards, let her fingers find his cheek. And as she had done weeks earlier with her mother, with Rick and her father, she explored the curve of his chin, the shape of his mouth, the contours of his nose, and the light wrinkles that creased his forehead. An index finger stopped at his left eyebrow. "Red?"

"Dark auburn," he said.

Impulsively, she grabbed his hand, then, and kissed it. "If I could just see—"

"You'll see before long," Rick interrupted. "Here comes Mum."

When her mother bent over and kissed her cheek, Debbie knew she'd been crying. She put her arm round her mother's neck and hugged her close. "I'm all right, Mum," she said. "Mr Griffin—"

"Mike," he broke in.

"—Mike brought me down—Mike and Rick."

"I know." Her voice was low and muffled. "Are you hurt anywhere? I know you're freezing."

"I'm not hurt. But Uncle Walt is."

"They're getting ready to take him to the hospital. Aunt Eva's with him. And they'll take you—"

"No, ma'am."

Eth pulled away. "No?"

"I'm going to the hospital Monday. I don't need to go now. And besides, I don't want to ride in anything. Not *anything*. All I want to do is sit and sit and sit. Where it's warm. And have a cup of hot, hot cocoa." She removed one arm from round her mother's neck and extended it. "Mike?"

He caught the hand, held it softly in his own. "Right here, Debbie."

"I never did have to thank anybody for saving my life before."

120

"Now's no time to start," he said. "You just rest. Just take it easy."

"Promise me something?"

"All right—what?"

"When I can see again, promise me you'll come to the hospital. I want you to be one of the first people I really can look at."

"I promise. And now I want you to promise *me* something."

"What?"

"When you're all well, you come out here and let me teach you how to fly—"

"I don't think I'll ever want to go up in a plane again."

"Sure you will. You're nearly a pilot now—won't take much more and you'll be able to handle a plane like Alice."

"I don't know," Debbie said slowly.

"I do," Mike said, and she could tell by the sound of his voice that he was halfway smiling.

Just then another man came to the side of her stretcher and leaned over. "Debbie," the voice said, "We've got a phone call for you."

"A *what?*"

"Some man's waiting for you to return his call. Said his name is Jeff Billings—"

"Oh! Oh, *him!*" She clutched her mother's arm. "Get me to a phone quick as you can! He was the first one to hear me on the radio. But," and she hesitated, "how'd he know I was—you know?"

"The news," Rick said. "You've been on the news."

Half an hour later, resting in a huge chair in Hans' office, warmed by the temperature in the room and by the hot cocoa her mother brought her, Debbie held the phone to her ear and waited for the operator to get Captain Billings on the line.

When he said hello, she tried to think of something original to say. She could not. "It's Debbie, Captain Billings—"

"I told you to call me Jeff. And, hey, you're something else!"

"Well," Debbie felt herself blushing, "I sure do thank you for helping me. I don't know what I'd have done—"

"Us pilots have to stick together," he said, interrupting her. "And I understand the doctors are going to clear up that eye problem for you."

"How'd you know that?"

"Oh—let's say I've been doing some checking up."

"Well, they're going to try."

"They'll do it—count on it. 'Cause I am. You tell 'em they've got to have you all well and seeing twenty-twenty by December twenty-ninth."

Debbie made a face. "What's that supposed to mean?"

"It means I'm going to Birmingham to see the Hall of Fame Bowl game. It means I'm flying a planeload of people down for it. And it means that you and that brother of yours are going to be my special guests—right on the fifty-yard line." He paused a moment. "That is, if your mother and father won't mind."

"Hey, that'll be great. And I know my parents won't mind. I'll see you then." And as she said it, she suddenly realized that she was no longer afraid of Monday, no longer afraid of the hospital, of the doctors, or of the operation. Her voice had a quickening sound to it when she added, "I mean, I *really will see you then* . . ."